Th[illegible] was in trouble. Bogg[illegible]-swept country, harried by ghostly Mormon raiders, short of rations, without mounts, and commanded by fat-headed, hide-bound brass, it didn't have a chance.

Except one.

That chance's name was Dan Spencer. He knew the country like he knew his rifle, he had tricks to beat blizzards, he could smell a raider or an Indian through a stand of pine.

He knew where he was and what to do.

Only, last year the Army had kicked him out . . .

SPECIAL MESSAGE TO READERS

THE ULVERSCROFT FOUNDATION
(registered UK charity number 264873)
was established in 1972 to provide funds for research, diagnosis and treatment of eye diseases. Examples of major projects funded by the Ulverscroft Foundation are:-

- The Children's Eye Unit at Moorfields Eye Hospital, London
- The Ulverscroft Children's Eye Unit at Great Ormond Street Hospital for Sick Children
- Funding research into eye diseases and treatment at the Department of Ophthalmology, University of Leicester
- The Ulverscroft Vision Research Group, Institute of Child Health
- Twin operating theatres at the Western Ophthalmic Hospital, London
- The Chair of Ophthalmology at the Royal Australian College of Ophthalmologists

You can help further the work of the Foundation by making a donation or leaving a legacy. Every contribution is gratefully received. If you would like to help support the Foundation or require further information, please contact:

THE ULVERSCROFT FOUNDATION
The Green, Bradgate Road, Anstey
Leicester LE7 7FU, England
Tel: (0116) 236 4325

website: www.foundation.ulverscroft.com

WINTER AMBUSH

E. E. HALLERAN

First published in Great Britain by Hammond
First published in the United States by Macrae Smith

First Isis Edition
published 2015
by arrangement with
Golden West Literary Agency

*A catalogue record for this book is available
from the British Library.*

ISBN 978–1–78541–002–4 (pb)

Published by
F. A. Thorpe (Publishing)
Anstey, Leicestershire

Set by Words & Graphics Ltd.
Anstey, Leicestershire
Printed and bound in Great Britain by
T. J. International Ltd., Padstow, Cornwall

This book is printed on acid-free paper

CHAPTER ONE

The two men in Buckskins Labored in silence to thwart the eddy that wanted to ground their clumsy flatboat beneath the sandy bluff. Then the craft shot back into the swift main channel and the long, angular man in the bow turned his hatchet profile to grimace at his younger and stockier companion.

"Big Muddy musta wanted us to jine the army," he said, black whiskers puckering around his grin. "Looked like we'd git shoved smack bang into Fort Leavenworth."

The younger man's brief nod acknowledged the humor. He was studying the sprawling encampment which topped the bluff on the Missouri's west bank. He was also heavily bearded and his patched and stained buckskins hinted at long, hard wear. The lounging sentries on the riverbank would not need to notice the flatboat's load of furs to realize that here was a pair of mountain men heading for market.

The gaunt man's smile faded as he followed his companion's thoughtful glance. "What d'ye make of it, Danny?" he asked. "Helluva lot o' sojers around the fort. Ye think them Kansas troubles have busted out worse?"

Dan Spencer nodded again, but he did not reply for a long minute. He was studying the familiar lines of the military post. Leavenworth itself was still the same sturdy outwork of civilization that it had been for years. The problem was posed by the encampment on the adjacent reservation. There were long lines of tents, orderly squares of freight wagons, a few newly built corrals, an artillery park, and temporary stables. Men were everywhere, some drilling in neat blue files, some working around wagons or buildings, some idling in the warmth of the May afternoon.

"I don't figure it's the Free State-Pro-Slave mess," he said finally, his words slowly thoughtful. "That'd mean a lot of patrols over a wide area. This looks like the gathering of a big expedition of some sort." A drawling quality in his voice did not quite conceal the background of education.

"Mebbe we kin go ashore at the town and ask a few questions," the lean man suggested hopefully.

Spencer chuckled. "Gettin' anxious for your annual toot, are you? Can't wait to reach St. Louis?"

"Aw, Danny, I ain't —"

"All right, McGee. Maybe we'll try Leavenworth. With all this up-river traffic in army supplies there ought to be a lot of empty boats going down. A smart fur buyer would set up shop in Leavenworth this year. We might get a better price than Callahan would offer."

McGee looked up quickly, his grin breaking out when he saw that his partner meant what he said. Then he turned back to study the collection of river craft which lined the sand bank below the next series of bluffs. Just as the fort had been erected on an elevation which would keep it clear of the Missouri's treacherous currents, so the town had been located. Now it was evident that the concentration of troops had turned the frontier village into a boom camp. Steamboats, keelboats and other craft jammed the strip of sand below the cut banks while a steady stream of wagons moved back and forth between the landing and various prairie camps.

"We kin shove in alongside that near side-wheeler," McGee called back. "Plenty o' room fer our size — and a low bank."

Spencer nodded without speaking, putting powerful shoulders into the task of shoving the boat out of the current and into the slack water above the line of beached river craft. The pair of them accomplished their purpose neatly enough, driving the blunt nose of the boat up on the sand in a twisting, slithering lunge that looked awkward but which was completely efficient. When a couple of lines were made fast to a convenient stump, the flatboat was safe.

The lines of stevedores unloading the side-wheeler eyed them without stopping work, but the mate of the steamer leaned over the rail to watch them with frank curiosity. He was joined by a young woman whose plain gray bonnet almost concealed her face. Once she turned her head so that a gleam of sunlight danced on fair hair and Spencer saw that she was quite pretty. It was only a fleeting impression, however, and when he looked up again she had disappeared.

There were still a few fleeting rays of sunshine left when all chores were complete. With the declining sun it was apparent that there was a corresponding slackening in the tempo of river-front activity. A gang of black roustabouts left the steamer, leaving only a half dozen hard-looking characters to haul a few odd packages up the bluff to a waiting wagon.

"Wanta toss up fer it?" McGee asked abruptly.

Spencer shook his head. He knew exactly what his partner wanted, but he didn't propose to let him get started. "Grub first," he said. "I'll get it. After supper it'll be your turn."

McGee didn't argue. He waved a rueful paw as Spencer started to open one of the fur bales. "Have it yore way — but don't git no idees if'n ye meet up with any stray pelt buyers. We're holdin' out fer twenty-four hunnert."

Spencer pulled a couple of pelts from the bale and refastened the rawhide thong. Then he started toward the beach, not even looking toward McGee as he said, "We'll do all right if we get two thousand. Beaver's off lately."

He climbed the sandy bank to the upper level, pausing to get his bearings before striding away toward the south. Dusk was beginning to close down but he knew that the main part of town was in that direction. Lights were beginning to gleam in windows while a rising tide of sound hinted that men were turning from labor to more enjoyable activities. Leavenworth must be a rip-roarer with all this army business on hand.

Three minutes' walk brought him to a general store which appeared to be part of the old town. A bald man with a fringe of ginger-colored whiskers and brown calf-eyes came forward to stare appraisingly at the worn buckskins and long hair of the stranger.

"Evenin'," the man said mildly. "Jest in from the mountains?"

"Half hour ago," Spencer told him. "Kinda hungry for some of the grub we ain't tasted in months. Trade for pelts?" He swung the two beaver skins to the counter between them.

The brown eyes didn't even blink, but the man's smile widened a trifle. "Been keepin' store here quite a spell, trapper. Pelts is money with me."

"How much money?"

"Reg'lar market. I ain't a speculator. That pair is what I'd call average fair." He pushed a broad finger against an item on a rather lengthy list posted on a pillar. "Market's low but steady. I don't reckon it'll change much this year."

Spencer studied the list, realizing that it covered many types of furs in all grades. Apparently he had been right in his guess that beaver was dropping. Two thousand would be just about top hope for this season.

"Looks like you know what you're talking about," he said. "That list has been up there a while — or do you just have it to scare trappers?"

The storekeeper smiled again. "I ain't speculatin'," he repeated. "Ask anybody."

"I'll take your word. Get me a pound of coffee, a pound of bacon, anything that'll eat like bread, some preserves or canned fruit. You must know what I want as well as I do."

"I oughta. Fresh bread from the bakery. Some butter what ain't half bad. Grape jam. Pickles. Mebbe a bit o' real decent cheese —"

"Get 'em. I got eating time to make up."

The exchange seemed to put them on a friendly basis and the storekeeper gossiped easily while putting up the purchases. Spencer learned that the army encamped outside the fort was scheduled to move west as a full-scale expedition to Utah. There had been trouble between United States officials and the Mormon leaders, trouble so serious that the government had decided to occupy the territory with the military.

"Government must be getting touchy," Spencer commented. "All I heard last fall was that Brigham Young's boys had flung out some crooked Federal judges."

"More to it than that," the storekeeper replied uneasily. "But I'm here to do business, not to talk politics."

Spencer did not press him. He went out into the darkness, swinging wide to take a look at the town before going back to the boat. The move brought a quick surprise. He had not gone a hundred yards when a familiar booming voice called his name. He turned to find a heavy man bearing down on him with outstretched hand. Even in the darkness there was a familiar quality about the broad form.

"Anvil Callahan!" he shouted, grabbing the big hand. "What brings you to Leavenworth?"

Mr. Callahan's rich Irish brogue erupted into a torrent of sound and out of it Spencer was able to discover that Callahan had moved his fur-buying activities to Leavenworth. Also, the Irishman's freight wagons were now pretty well concentrated at the fort while government contracts were being carried out.

"I could use ye, Danny-b'y," Callahan said. "We'll be needin' ivery good wagonman we kin git. Good wages this summer for a gossoon what'll stop gaddin' about and drive a team west."

Spencer shook his head. "Sorry, Anvil. You know my summer program is always full."

There was a moment of silence and it seemed that Callahan would ask a question, but instead he forced a laugh. "It's yer own business, Danny. But don't fergit if ye change yer mind. Bring any pelts down the river?"

"Don't I always? Mormon McGee and me. Above town a bit, next to the last big steamboat."

"I'll be along early in the mornin'. Prices ain't very high though."

"So I understand. Now I'll get back and feed McGee. He'll be off on one of his sprees before the night's over, but I'll send him out with a full belly."

"Then ye don't want to talk price now?"

"You know I don't. You set 'em. I trust you."

"That's the trouble with ye, Danny. Ye make me ashamed to cheat ye."

"Exactly," Spencer agreed with a chuckle. "See you tomorrow."

He was feeling much more at peace with the world when he turned away and headed for the flatboat. A brush with Callahan helped a man to forget the resentment which had come from sight of the army post.

A lantern was bobbing around on the flatboat when he groped his way down the bank to the sand flat. He realized that two men were aboard the craft, one of them inspecting the cargo. Evidently Callahan was not the only fur buyer in town.

He was about to make himself known when a voice came to his ears. "What'll yuh take for the whole load, trapper?" The heavy rasp of it seemed familiar and Spencer frowned in the darkness, trying to think.

McGee's reply came clearly. "Three thousand flat."

Spencer chuckled silently, amused at the brisk attitude McGee was adopting.

The deeper voice rumbled, "A mite over the market, friend. How would two thousand sound?"

Spencer could make out the fur buyer now. The man was broad of shoulder and heavily built all over. A frock coat and a broad-brimmed hat were distinguishable in the light of the lantern and again Spencer had a feeling that he ought to know the fellow.

"Don't hardly sound at all," McGee said. "Seems like a real puny number. Can't even hear it."

"Twenty-two hundred?"

A tone of scented triumph sounded in the McGee voice as he countered. "Seein' as how ye're Johnny on the spot, mister, I'll let ye have the lot fer twenty-eight hunnert."

"You're no trapper. You're a bandit. I'll give twenty-four."

Spencer's interest picked up. His own impression of the market, the price list at the trading post, and the remarks of Callahan made him feel that two thousand would be top price. Why was this man going well above the true market value?

"Twenty-six," McGee said.

The big man laughed. "Now I suppose you'll expect me to split the difference and take twenty-five?"

"Nope. I like to dicker but I ain't payin' a hunnert dollars fer havin' that kind o' fun. Twenty-six, take it or leave it."

"I'll take it. Suppose I meet you here after breakfast tomorrow mornin' and we'll go up to the express company's office to make settlement. My men will take charge of the load then. Shake on it?"

McGee obliged him and the big man turned away with a parting injunction. "The deal's made. We agree on that, don't we?"

"I shook with ye, didn't I?" McGee snapped, sounding almost aggrieved in spite of the triumph he could not quite conceal.

"Then good evenin' to you."

Spencer caught a glimpse of a broad, smoothly shaven face in the flicker of a lantern and then the fur buyer was gone, leaving the partners to face each other silently. They waited until the sound of footsteps on the sand had died away and then McGee asked, "Did ye git back in time to hear the dicker?"

"I heard most of it. Who was he?"

McGee cackled in jubilation. "Name's Catlett. Did ye hear how I got the uneven split outa him?"

"I heard." Spencer wasn't trying to dull the edge of his partner's victory. He simply felt certain that something was wrong.

"Callahan's in Leavenworth," he said. "I talked to him."

"Didn't make no deal, did ye?"

"No. He'll be along in the morning."

"Think he'll up Catlett's bid?"

"I don't think he'll offer as much."

"Then we don't do no business with Anvil this year. Right?"

"We'll see. Now get a fire built and we'll try to fill your belly to a point where you can't hold enough liquor to do you too much damage."

CHAPTER TWO

An hour passed before McGee trudged away toward the rising tumult of revelry which marked the town. He had not attempted to defend his own reputation against the half-joking remarks Spencer aimed at him, but he became almost sullen when his bargaining ability was questioned.

"I still think something's wrong," Spencer told him flatly. "That jasper offered too much. Ask around a bit and see what prices are like."

"I'll ask," McGee agreed, "but I still figger we got a deal. I caught a easy mark what don't know the trade too good."

Spencer turned to the task of preparing for the night. A boatload of prime pelts would always be a temptation to thieves, and Leavenworth would be certain to have its share of hard cases. The lighted steamboat would afford a certain amount of protection for the next few hours. When the boat's lights went out would be the time for a man to keep his guard up.

He brought a pair of pistols out of a box, studying them a bit grimly as he tested their balance. They were not as modern as some of the new revolvers coming on the market, but they bore the name of Samuel Colt and had seen good service in Texas. For a close fight Spencer wanted nothing better.

He cleaned and polished the weapons, content to work in the dim light from the side-wheeler. While his fingers operated automatically at the task, his mind was busy with the puzzle of the strange fur dealer. He tried vainly to make his memory identify that oddly familiar figure. Then he suddenly recalled the voice once more and knew. After nine years of searching for a face, he had let his ears get off guard and had failed to recognize the voice that went with it.

"Catlett, hell!" he said, half aloud in sudden anger at his own stupidity. "That was Curt Donnel with his whiskers shaved off!"

He stood up quickly, the twin Colts gripped tightly in hands that seemed ready to crush the steel butts. So he had caught up with Donnel at last! He took a single stride toward shore but then caught himself up with a grunt. What was to be gained by a hasty move now? Donnel would be back. That overly generous offer was beginning to make a lot of vicious sense.

Bitter thoughts crowded Spencer's mind as he forced himself to do a calm job of loading the six-guns. Donnel was within reach at last — but what was to be done about it? In nine years of searching he had never come up with any sort of real plan of action. All he had tried to do was to find Donnel, hoping that when the time came some way would present itself. For the moment he could see no such prospect.

His preoccupation did not keep him from noting a tap of heels on the nearby deck of the side-wheeler. It made him think of the fair-haired girl he had glimpsed so briefly just at dusk, and he found himself wondering about her. She hadn't seemed like the sort of woman to be found on the frontier. As the thought crossed his mind his ear told him that she was walking toward the steamer's gangplank, heading ashore — alone. Maybe she was not as gentle as she had seemed.

To his surprise, however, she did not climb the bank after leaving the freight deck, but turned in the semidarkness to approach the flatboat. In the gleam of the lights he could make out a trim figure swathed in a long cape while a gleam of gold told him that tonight she was bareheaded.

"May I come aboard your boat, sir?" she called quietly, the query as calm as though this were an ordinary social occasion. It was not only the serene dignity of the voice which caught his attention; her accent stamped her immediately as English and rather well educated.

"Make yourself right at home," he invited after a moment of surprised hesitation.

She wasted no words, halting as soon as she spotted him in the gloom. Her words were precise and to the point. "You are a trapper down from the Rocky Mountains, I believe. Do you know the road to Utah?"

Again he found himself hesitating in astonishment. "I'm a trapper, ma'am," he said, "and I'm just outa the hills — but there's no road to Utah. Not even a decent kind of trail."

"Do you know that trail?"

"I've been over it a couple of times. This end of it often."

"Could you guide wagons to Utah Territory?"

"If I wanted to."

"You do not make it easy for me," she said, a shade of impatience creeping into the calm voice. "I wish to reach Utah without delay. I am willing to pay more than the usual rate of wages to a competent man who will take two wagons through. Naturally I will also hire whatever helpers my guide will require."

"You're offering me the job?"

"That was my intention."

"Why did you pick me? You don't know a thing about me."

"I fear I am in no position to be too careful. Frankly, I have been eavesdropping ever since you arrived here this afternoon. I heard you refer to your partner as Mormon. That suggested that you might have knowledge of Utah. Tonight I listened to some of your conversation and came to the conclusion that you are capable and probably trustworthy. Will you accept?"

"You want an answer right away?"

"Naturally."

"Then it's no."

"May I ask why?"

"Of course. The reason is that I don't go into anything blind. I know there's an army heading for Utah this summer, but I don't know much about the hows or whys of it. To me it means that anybody else on the trail is likely to get tangled up with the military. It could be awkward."

"You don't think I'm a spy or something equally ridiculous, do you?"

Suddenly he felt a little ashamed of evading the issue. For nine long years he had been trying to force a showdown with Curt Donnel and only tonight had he gotten close enough to the man to have any hope of success. No job would take him away from Leavenworth until he could follow up the Donnel matter — and it might take all summer. So why let this girl talk just because it was pleasant to hear her?

"Sorry I made it sound that way," he said shortly. "Let's leave it *this* way: I'm not going to Utah."

"Then your partner? Would he feel the same way?"

"Hard to tell. But don't count on learning much from him for a few days. He won't be sober enough to talk."

"Thank you." The words were polite enough, but the tone was almost bitter as she turned away toward the steamer gangplank. Spencer wanted to call after her and make some sort of apology for his brusqueness but thought better of it and remained silent. There could be no point in prolonging the interview. Better to get her out of the way so he could focus his thoughts on the troubles which he now felt certain were scheduled for tonight.

Spencer sat in the shadows a long time after the girl's brisk footsteps ceased to click on the steamer's deck. Mostly he kept his mind on the subject of Curt Donnel, but it was very easy for thoughts to stray to the blonde girl who had been so insistent upon starting for Utah. He kept wondering why she wanted to go and why she was so apparently desperate about it. He knew that there had been a veritable tide of European converts streaming toward the Mormon settlements during the past couple of years, but he also knew that most of these folks were unfortunates of one sort or another who saw the fabulous land of milk and honey beyond the mountains as an escape from poverty in the old country. The blonde girl did not fit that description at all.

He forced the puzzle from his mind and presently found himself able to concentrate on the less pleasant matter of Curt Donnel. There was a perverse sort of whimsy about the thoughts, he realized. After all these years of bitterness, trailing Donnel with no real plan in mind but only the hope that somehow the man could be made to talk, now Donnel was close at hand — but in the role of hunter instead of hunted. Spencer could not plan a campaign against the man; he had to be ready to defend himself against him.

At least that was the way the deal seemed to line up. A real fur buyer might have been foolish enough or inexperienced enough to make an offer that was far above the market. But not Curt Donnel. In his long career as a thief, smuggler and general outlaw, Donnel had been accused of many things, but no one had ever suggested that he was stupid. Donnel must have had a good reason for making his offer — and Spencer believed that he knew what that reason would be. The whole idea was to keep the boatload of furs at this spot — out of the hands of any legitimate dealer — until the Donnel brand of piracy could go into operation.

A glance at the stars told Spencer that the hour was getting late. Midnight could not be far away. In another hour the town would settle itself to something that resembled quiet. Already the steamer's lights were going out one by one and soon the entire river front would be darkly silent, a perfect spot for the sort of work Donnel understood so well. His bully-boys would launch their attack under cover of darkness, hoping to dispose of any boat occupants before an alarm could be raised. After that the flatboat would be shoved out into the current and permitted to drift downstream to some spot where its load could be transferred to another craft. Meanwhile, its late owners would be carried along beneath the whirling water until somewhere along the lower river an unidentifiable corpse would be found. Other unwary trappers had disappeared in the same manner.

Finally the side-wheeler doused its last lantern and Spencer moved into action. He had been studying the top of the bluff but could not see any indication of a watcher up there. Still he played it as cautiously as possible, assuming that Donnel's gang would have a scout posted. Working quietly, he shoved a couple of fur bales into position and made room for himself behind them. After that he rechecked the caps on his twin Colts and settled down to wait.

He wondered briefly whether Donnel would come with his hatchet men but decided that it would not be likely. Donnel was too smart to put himself in the danger spot and would prefer to handle whatever arrangements would be made downstream. Spencer was satisfied to have it so; he didn't want to risk losing Donnel. Killing the man would only choke off the possibility of getting him to talk.

Waiting in the darkness of the moonless night was dull, and twice Spencer caught himself nodding. He had been on the move since dawn and now he had to fight sleep without making any movement which might betray his position.

An hour passed drearily enough, only an occasional yell from the distant saloon district reminding the watcher that men were still awake and active. Maybe that fact would keep any attack from developing just yet. He almost hoped it wouldn't; he would have preferred to get the crisis over before his tired eyes shut completely. He even tried to switch his thoughts back to the English girl, but even that didn't seem to help much. The only scheme that seemed to do any good was to sit in such an uncomfortable position that the discomfort kept him awake.

Then a figure moved stealthily on the top of the bluff and Spencer was suddenly wide awake and testing the hammers of his guns. He listened breathlessly, trying to determine whether this might be a scout from the probable raiding party or merely Mormon McGee trying to find his way back to the boat. The sound was not repeated and after a while Spencer told himself that he had dreamed it in the first place.

He was not conscious that the reaction lowered his alertness, but the next sound was close at hand, actually aboard the flatboat. Instantly he knew that he had been asleep. Someone was close beside him. Maybe it was McGee and maybe it wasn't.

A man grunted irritably as he stumbled against a bale of pelts, but still Spencer could not identify the fellow. It might be McGee, more than half drunk and blundering against the bales which had been moved to form a defense position. From the first Spencer had planned to be in a position to recognize an intruder before he could board the boat. That nap had ruined the whole plan. The intruder — if he was one — was already within four feet.

Spencer decided to risk a challenge. "That you, Mormon?" he asked sharply.

The answer came in a pair of grunts, one of surprise and then one of affirmation. It was the sort of reply McGee might have given and for an instant it threw Spencer off guard. In that instant a burly shadow hurled itself at him, hurdling the bundle of furs which had concealed him.

There was no time to aim a gun. Spencer used his right-hand weapon as a club, partly blocking the attack and at the same time trying to strike home a hard but short blow at his assailant. He knew that he had brought a new kind of grunt from the other man but only at the cost of being driven backward across a locker.

Something ripped at the sleeve of his buckskin jacket so he twisted hard, trying to avoid the knife of the attacker and at the same time get into a position where he could use his free hand. For a moment the other man pinned him down, evidently trying for a strangle hold with one hand to prevent an outcry. Spencer ignored the fingers clawing at his beard; the danger was that knife in the man's other hand.

Somewhere at the far end of the boat a voice hailed in a hoarse whisper, "Got 'im, Schlagel?"

There was no time for any reply. An arm went up in a vicious arc, starlight winked on polished steel. Spencer saw it and managed to intercept the blow with his left hand, rolling as he did so and smashing the right-hand gun into the face of the man above him. When the fellow cursed and faltered, Spencer seized the initiative, twisting the captured knife arm and hammering in again with the gun. The sound of metal against flesh told him that he had smashed his antagonist's nose, but there was no time to think about details. Two more shadows were closing in from the other end of the flatboat.

Spencer stepped back from the man who was now slumping in front of him. There was no pursuit from that worthy, so Spencer used his moment of respite to change his tactics. Noise was what these bandits did not want, so he'd provide some noise.

He drove a shot in low, aiming hastily at the bulk of the nearer of the two attackers. It brought a smothered yell of alarm but not of pain, so he fired again, this time taking better aim. The man went down and Spencer turned his gun on number three, blasting two shots in quick succession. It was blind shooting, but he was more interested in making plenty of noise and the strategy brought quick results. From the shore a voice hailed in peremptory command, "Git back here, dam' ye! We got to run fer it."

Spencer turned to drive a slug in the direction of the voice and his action provided the men aboard the boat with sufficient time for a hasty retreat. He could have picked any one of them off as they clambered ashore over the bow, but he held his fire. It was enough to know that two of them were moving clumsily and in apparent pain. For good measure he emptied the gun in the general direction of the man who had remained on the shore, then shifted to the other weapon. That ought to take care of matters for a while. No point in having the local law take a hand because of a dead bandit or two lying around.

By that time lights were flashing aboard the steamboat and someone was bawling lustily for help. Spencer grinned in the darkness. Evidently a sleepy crewman on watch was under the impression that river pirates were attacking the side-wheeler.

He waited until a man appeared at the steamer's hurricane deck rail. "Fur pirates," he said shortly. "Tried to jump me while I slept."

Another man appeared beside the first one, looking ridiculous in a blue uniform coat and a nightcap. "What happened to 'em?" he demanded, an edge of suspicion in his voice.

Spencer shrugged. "Send a man down with a torch and we'll look around. I'm kinda curious to see if I drew blood from any of the polecats."

A hail from the high ground interrupted him and he swung around with his gun ready. Even now there was no point in being careless.

“I’m comin’ aboard, Spencer,” the newcomer yelled. “Don’t git no brash idees with that shootin’ iron.”

A dozen people were yelling questions from the steamboat now and presently a deck hand ran out over the bow with a torch, the nightcapped officer at his heels. The two were just in time to meet a thickset man in buckskins who half rolled down the steep bank to the sand flat. He seemed to be carrying a sizeable load of liquor, but he managed to regain his feet and assume the duty of interpreting the sign which the torch disclosed on the sand.

“I was jest in time to hear the end of it,” he told the officer. “Looks like fur thieves, all right. Looky here. Four *hombres* talked together close up. Then three of ’em sneaked aboard the flatboat. Here’s where they hustled off again, one of ’em draggin’ a foot like he was hurt. Blood spots on the sand here and here and here.”

The noisy investigation dragged on for another fifteen minutes, but it might as well have ended right there. The man in buckskins had told the whole story, so far as the evidence went. There were other smears of fresh blood aboard the flatboat, while a long-bladed knife was discovered beside one of the fur bales. Presently the steamboaters went away and their ship relapsed into darkness and quiet once more. Spencer found himself wondering what the English girl had thought of the night’s events. Maybe she would be having some doubts about trailing off to Utah with the kind of men to be met along the Big Muddy.

The stranger introduced himself. “I’m Cal Trent, Spencer. McGee told me where to find yuh. He’s in the calaboose.”

Spencer nodded. “Sounds normal. What did he do this time?”

Trent was dragging a couple of fur bales into line, clearly intending to stretch out on them. “Nuthin’ much,” he replied, easing himself down. “Me and him — and a couple of other fellers — got to braggin’ about the rip-roarin’ times we used to have around Santy Fee and one thing led to another till — say, this ain’t such a bad pallet fer a tired ole man.”

“Till what?”

“Well, purty soon Mormon gits to braggin’ about his shootin’ eye. Dang fool took a pistol off’n a provost guard to prove hisself. That’s when they hauled him off to the pokey. G’night now, Spencer. We’ll git McGee out come daylight.” A tentative snore hinted that Mr. Trent had completed his explanation.

CHAPTER THREE

Spencer rubbed thoughtfully at the tender spot on his throat where the thug's fingers had clawed. Then he grinned a little in the darkness. He had heard of Cal Trent and his reputation for garrulous eccentricity, but it still seemed odd to have a man come upon a scene of excitement — and with gossip of his own to retail — only to fall asleep uninvited on another man's property.

Not that it mattered much. Trent was welcome and the story of McGee could wait. At the moment Spencer was more concerned with working out a plan to trap Curt Donnel. After the failure of his attack, the fellow probably would be wary, but he still would not know that the man who had beaten off his thugs was anything more than another trapper.

He sifted plans for the better part of an hour without coming up with anything that sounded halfway smart. Then he fell asleep.

He awoke to find the sun in his eyes and a gang of roustabouts already hauling freight over the gangplank of the side-wheeler. Cal Trent snored lustily on his improvised cot, a stocky, untidy-looking fellow whose round features looked almost cherubic in spite of his matted gray beard. Spencer went ashore alone and built a fire and prepared a substantial breakfast from leftovers of the night's feast. Then he went back aboard the flatboat and shook Trent.

"Grub's on the fire, Trent," he announced as the bloodshot eyes opened to stare at him with instant alertness.

"Ready," Trent told him, rolling to a sitting position. "Seems as if a man gits good service in this here ho-tel."

"I'll put in an extra charge on your bill," Spencer said.

Suddenly Trent slipped out of his jacket and boosted himself to the rail of the flatboat. Almost in the same movement he went over backward into the river, immersing the upper half of his body with his knees hooked over the gunwale. Then he came up again to sit erect, gasping a little as he slapped at wet hide. The agility of the move was almost as surprising as the sight of a mountain man taking a bath.

Neither man had much to say until they were well along with their morning meal. Then Trent said abruptly, "Ain't got no call to worry; he'll be all right."

"What's that?" Spencer's question was sharp. He had been thinking about Curt Donnel and the statement caught him by surprise.

"Mormon won't be in the pokey long," Trent explained patiently. "Cap Marcy'll see to that."

"Who's Marcy?"

"He'll be lookin' ye up. Soon's he gits Mormon out."

Spencer wanted to pursue the matter further but the arrival of Anvil Callahan interrupted the prospect of unraveling the Trent style of explanation. Callahan came down from the bluff with mixed emotions showing in his big red face. Obviously he was excited, but Spencer thought he could detect something like relief in the look as well. Probably Anvil had heard some news of the night's battle.

In daylight it was easy to guess how the man had gotten his nickname. In spite of the fact that he matched Spencer's six feet, he looked out of proportion because of his enormously wide shoulders. Only when he removed the broad-brimmed hat did the full meaning of the name become clear. From temple to temple a shining fringe of violently red hair encircled a shiny bald spot. Matt Clancy, Callahan's best friend and present wagon boss, had once likened the sight to a glowing horseshoe on an anvil. Callahan had been Anvil ever since.

"Who jumped ye, Danny?" he greeted explosively. "And are ye all right?"

"Listen to him, Trent," Spencer gibed. "Sounds like he was worried about me when anybody would know that all he cared about was making sure he had a chance to cheat me on a fur deal before some other robber could beat him to it."

"The tongue of him!" Callahan exploded. "Silent Spencer they call him, but fer me he jist rattles all the time."

"Self-defense," Spencer explained solemnly. "With McGee I can just let him talk. With you I have to beat you down a bit to save my ears."

"Always blackguardin'," Calahan growled. "I dunno fer the life o' me why I iver git near ye."

"Generally because you want something," Spencer said. "I'm just an easy mark for a big, dumb Irishman so you always come around to take advantage of my good nature. What kind of skin game are you planning this time?"

Trent swallowed the last of his bacon and wiped his greasy hands on the leg of his pants. "Good friends, I take it?" he suggested.

"While I got him in front o' me where I kin be watchin' the beast," Callahan rumbled.

Suddenly he seemed to feel that there had been enough of the badinage. "Did a dandy gossoon named Catlett see ye last evenin', Danny?" he asked, his tone completely sober.

"He saw McGee," Spencer explained. "Made him quite an offer while I was in town."

"I shoulda warned ye, Danny. What happened after that?"

Spencer showed him the gash in the sleeve of his jacket. "This — and some minor contusions on the other side. Do I understand that you're wise to the game our friend is playing?"

"We been gittin' mighty suspicious-like, but we ain't had a chance to prove a thing on him. Mostly the men we want to see have disappeared." It was noteworthy that Anvil Callahan lost most of his heavy brogue when he became serious.

"I can understand why."

"I don't," Trent put in. "What are ye gabbin' about anyhow?"

"The first part of what you saw last night," Spencer told him. "It seems that there is a bit of competition between fur buyers here in Leavenworth. The worthy Mr. Callahan prefers to rob his victims in a gentlemanly style, burying them under a load of blarney while he steals them blind. It annoys him that some other pirate has adopted unethical methods. This man who calls himself Catlett — but who has had other names in the past — uses simpler devices. He makes a big offer in a hurry so that a trapper will not sell to a swindler like Callahan. While the furs are being held for him he sends a gang of cut-throats to grab the load and dispose of the unfortunate owners. Mr. Callahan thinks it's unfair competition."

"Sure and it's a dirrty way ye have o' puttin it, Danny." Anvil grimaced. "How did ye manage to tumble in time?"

"Because I got a look at the man just as he was leaving. After a while I realized who he was and then it was easy. His reputation and the bid he made to McGee had to add up that way. Even then I let myself be caught napping."

"Not too much, I reckon," Callahan chuckled. "Me boys brung the word this mornin' early. One o' Catlett's wagons went out before daylight with a couple o' wounded men aboard. Sure and it's the chance I've been waitin' for to prove somethin' on that son of a banshee."

"What can you prove?" Spencer demanded. "Think it over."

Callahan was silently unhappy for several moments and Spencer went on in a grim tone. "I want that man — alive — so he can be made to talk. You can help by playing along and keeping a close track of him. Get all the information possible about him. Then leave him to me."

"But he'll —"

"He'll lay for a while, I imagine. Just play it my way. Now what about this load of pelts? When are your boys coming to get them?"

"Any minute now."

"Good. Put the money to my account and don't let McGee have more than ten dollars at a time unless I give you the word."

"Want to talk price?"

"We settled that last night. Just make it fair or I'll come back and haunt you."

Callahan guffawed. "So it's yerself will haunt *me!* Me what's thirty years ahead."

"The good die young," Spencer reminded him. "Which clears the way for you to plunder honest trappers for many years yet."

"Always the blatherskite!" Anvil growled. "But there's the boys now. Unload yer dirty bundles so workin' men kin handle their chores. I'll be gittin' back to the shop."

The rash of conversation ended abruptly with his departure. It was always so, Spencer thought with a grin. Something about Anvil Callahan always had a tongue-loosening effect. Maybe it was a good thing for a man to forget his silent habits once in a while.

He made two bundles of his personal property and that of McGee and turned Mormon's outfit over to Trent. By that time Callahan's crew was preparing to move the flatboat downstream and Spencer made only one comment to them. "Take care of the traps. Anvil will know what to do with 'em." Then he was on his way toward town, falling into step behind Trent. Now that the fur business was in good hands he could let his mind dwell on other matters.

At the top of the bluff he turned to look back over the scene and was instantly aware of the trim figure on the hurricane deck of the steamboat. The English girl was wearing the gray bonnet once more, but again he caught a glimpse of pleasant features and pale hair beneath it. She was looking straight at him but offered no sign of greeting or recognition, turning away quickly at his glance. He wondered how much of the morning's talk she had overheard. Probably enough to make her feel happy that she had not gotten into any sort of contract with him. It should have been a satisfying thought on his part — but it wasn't.

Trent broke a long silence when they were halfway through the town. "Sounds plain nasty to hit a man's weakness when it's honesty," he complained.

"How was that again?" Spencer asked. He had almost forgotten Trent's tendency to talk in riddles. "Whose weakness is honesty?"

"Anvil's. Me. I never tumbled to it."

"You know Callahan?"

"Sell my pelts to him every year. That's the hell of it."

"Don't you always get a square deal?"

"Sure. Everybody does with Callahan."

"What's the complaint then?"

"I jest woke up to how to beat the big Irishman. Every spring I dicker hard with him and every year he beats me. Jest now I see how ye do it. Let him set his own price and he gives ye what's right instead o' what ye'll settle fer. Sounds downright crooked. Wish I'd thought of it sooner."

They turned in at the immense log tavern which was one of the settlement's earliest structures. The Wagon Train had been named appropriately enough in the days when so many emigrants started away from the Missouri at that point, but now its trade was more varied.

A reek of stale whiskey and strong tobacco greeted Spencer and Trent as they went into a long room where a few men sat around idly, some of them spruced up for the day's activities and some merely getting over the effects of the previous night. Trent led the way toward an inner door and Spencer followed without comment. Evidently the room which had come to be a headquarters for the mountain men was still reserved for that purpose.

A half-dozen bearded individuals were still asleep in the barnlike apartment which was an addition to the original building. None of them stirred at the entry of the newcomers and Trent motioned toward an unoccupied cot. Spencer dumped his belongings there, retaining only a single revolver which he thrust into his belt beneath the buckskin jacket. Then he asked quietly, "You taking care of the McGee problem?"

Trent grinned. "Me and Cap Marcy."

"Good. I'll be back here along about evening. Try Anvil's place if you want me for anything before that time."

He left the Wagon Train at once, reflecting that it was something of a comfort to let other people handle some of the chores occasionally. He did not know why he was so willing to leave matters to a total stranger like Cal Trent, but somehow he knew that it would be all right. It even gave him a sort of glow to realize that he now had three friends in the vicinity. A man who had been so much on his own for so many years could appreciate it.

He found a general store close at hand and was inside before he realized that he did not have a copper in his pocket. So he asked, "Where do I find Anvil Callahan's place?"

The lantern-jawed storekeeper sized him up instantly. "Sell to Callahan?" he asked.

"About a half hour ago."

"He's along the river, mebbe three hundred yards that way. If it's credit ye want, I'll take an order on Anvil."

Spencer nodded easily. It was no surprise that the Callahan reputation should have become so quickly a part of Leavenworth commerce. On the frontier men learned quickly about such matters. "Suits me," he said.

When he left the store he was carrying a bundle that contained a pair of good quality gray trousers, a shirt of lightweight gray flannel, a pair of cavalry boots, socks, underwear, and a flat-crowned black hat like the one Callahan usually wore.

He took his new outfit down the dusty street a short distance and entered a barbershop. A bath, shave, and haircut made him feel a little less like a Blackfoot, and when he sallied forth once more in his new garments he bore scant resemblance to the mountain rat who had gone in. Aside from the fact that his nose was sunburned while his chin was white, he might have been considered a rather handsome young fellow. Without the beard his features showed pleasantly even, only the brooding gray eyes and the firm chin belying the overall impression of good nature.

Spencer had considered retaining the beard but had succumbed to the desire to let his face feel really clean again. The crop of whiskers might serve as a sort of disguise, but he did not believe that Donnel would recognize him anyway. The man had never known him too well and in the old days Spencer had worn a youthfully pompous mustache.

He found the Callahan headquarters to be a tiny shack flanked by a warehouse, a corral, and a large open space where a dozen immense freight wagons were standing. Anvil was alone in the shack and Spencer hailed him with a show of grim humor. "Any of your boys learn anything — or are they as stupid as their boss?"

Anvil glared from beneath bushy brows. "Palaverin' breshape!" he snorted. "Quit yer blackguardin' or I won't tell ye a dam' thing."

"No? When could a Callahan ever keep a secret?"

"Sit down and stop yer clackin' tongue. I got me boys on the chore right away. It looks like Donnel lit a shuck."

"Skipped town?"

"Mebbe. And then again mebbe not. I'm thinkin' he's slipped off to the army camp."

"Why?"

"Because he's thinkin' there'll be a stink after last night. At the same time he's got a deal on the fire there. Contracted fer a half-dozen wagons, I hear. I'd figger he thinks it's healthier to be an army wagoner than a fur trader fer a spell."

"Has he been handling any wagon trade here?"

"Some. Santa Fe trail, I hear. Some o' the boys figger he's handlin' smuggled stuff outa there and mebbe runnin' a few guns to the Mescaleros on the way back."

"Sounds like him. Does he keep a crew here at Leavenworth?"

"Nope. No outfit at all. Ginerally he hangs up around a saloon jist down the road a piece. His wagons come and go with their drivers takin' care o' the chores while they're on this end. We ain't sure how big a gang he's in with, but it's right fair size."

Spencer nodded without speaking. The setup suited him well enough. If Donnel was hooked up with some sort of organization it would be easier to keep him in sight, particularly since the man would not have any idea that he was being trailed.

Then he remembered something else. "Tell me one thing more. Last night you called our friend Catlett. Just now you referred to him as Donnel. How come?"

Callahan chuckled. "I been waitin' fer ye to ask that, even if'n it wasn't necessary. When ye didn't blink at the Donnel name I knowed I was on the right track."

"What track?"

"Yerself, me bucko. Didn't ye figger I'd get curious about ye? Every spring ye sell yer pelts and light out fer nobody knows where. Somethin' is eatin' at ye, everybody knows. Bein' as I like ye, in spite o' yer nasty disposition, and bein' as I'm jist naturally nosey, I started askin' questions. It wasn't long before I got me a few facts. The army threw a bad deal at ye back in the Mexican War and at the time ye claimed ye was hornswoggled by a bully-boy named Donnel. So I put two and two together after the way ye talked last evenin'. This here Donnel could be the crook who's now namin' hisself Catlett. Right?"

"Right," Spencer said.

"Jist so we understand each other," Callahan said placidly. "I'm on yer side, Danny. Ye know that. Now let's see if we can't cook up a few plans."

There was no time for planning. A young woman entered the shack, her manner hinting that she was embarrassed but determined. The gray bonnet and pale hair identified her at once and Spencer was interested to learn that he had not guessed wrongly in calling her pretty. Seeing her thus for the first time in daylight, he noted that her features were round enough to be pleasant but firm enough to fit well with the determination she had already expressed. Mostly, however, it was her eyes which marked her as a girl of strong character. She knew exactly what she was doing and she did not propose to let anything stand in the way.

"You are Mr. Callahan," she said, making it a statement rather than a question.

The burly Irishman stood up quickly, bowing with some awkwardness but withal courteously. "The same, ma'am. Would there be anything I could be doin' fer ye?"

"I would like to speak to you privately. About business." Her sidelong glance at Spencer indicated that she did not recognize him without the beard.

Spencer reached for his hat but Callahan stopped him with a gesture. "For private business, miss, ye'll do well to let my partner listen. He's a b'y with foine ideas. A little crazy sometimes, but interestin'."

She smiled briefly at the obvious show of humor. "I came to you because I heard you referred to as an honest man. You are in the freighting business, I believe." Again she stated rather than asked. Spencer reflected that she must have been listening to some of his talk with Trent. Probably that interview at the flatboat with Anvil had not been missed either. That was why she had been able to identify Callahan correctly when she entered the shack.

"I shall state my case briefly," she went on when Callahan made no reply. "I wish to reach Utah without delay. I own two wagons and am prepared to purchase the necessary stock to haul them. Would your company be prepared to provide me with teamsters and a guide for the journey?"

Anvil smothered his surprise but shook his head quickly. "Sorry, ma'am, but I don't reckon it'd work. Ivery wagon I've got is goin' to work on an army contract. That means I'll need ivery man jack I kin hire."

She was frankly disappointed, but she tried again. "Then could you suggest anyone else who might be in a position to assist me?"

"Not this season. This here army expedition has got the whole frontier tied up. Anyway, I'm doubtin' ye'd git through. Them b'ys in blue ain't lettin' much git through ahead of 'em."

"But it is most important that I make the journey."

"Likely so, ma'am, but I ain't got nary thing to offer. How about yerself, Danny?"

Spencer was not sure what was meant by the question, but the answer had to be in the negative. He contented himself with a shake of the head. As long as the girl had not recognized him he didn't propose to complicate matters by having her recognize his voice.

"Ye might try the army folks," Callahan suggested not too hopefully. "They might think of somethin'."

"Thank you," she said, turning to leave. Spencer had a feeling that, in her disappointment, she did not trust herself to speak further.

When she had drawn out of earshot, Callahan aimed a broad grin at his younger companion. "Ye should have taken the job, Danny. It'd sure be an entertainin' chore fer a handsome gossoon like yerself."

"She made me a proposition last night," Spencer told him dryly.

"Where?"

"At the flatboat. It seems she's been living aboard that steamer we moored beside. I've been curious about her, with that English accent and all, but not curious enough to get myself tangled up in a deal that will put me off Donnel's trail."

"She's a lot purtier'n Donnel," Anvil commented.

"And probably headed for Utah to become the fifth wife of some Mormon. Stop sounding romantic and use your head."

"You're too young to sound like that, Danny."

"I'm old enough to know what I'm doing. It's Donnel I'm after; anything else can wait."

CHAPTER FOUR

By midafternoon spencer felt that he was ready to concentrate on the Donnel matter. The routine chores of disposing of the pelts were complete and he had money in his pocket. McGee had been released and was asleep at the Wagon Train, more disgruntled over the failure of his deal with Catlett than at his personal misadventures.

Spencer was about to set out on a search of the camps when Cal Trent came into the Wagon Train accompanied by a wizened little trapper called Shorty and a sturdy-looking infantry officer of indeterminate age. The soldier's hair was shot with gray, but his neatly trimmed brown beard and keen eyes suggested that the gray was premature. He was well tanned but the shade of the tan seemed odd. It was yellowish rather than the normal brown of the prairie.

"Sit in, will ye?" Trent greeted. "We're havin' a meetin' in the back room. I'll git the fellers awake."

Spencer went along, nodding easily in return to the infantry captain's smile. The formalities were brief, Trent merely bellowing for the sleeping mountain men to wake up and listen. "Cap Marcy," he announced, jerking a brown thumb toward the visitor. "Commander of the scout company. Shorty and me is helpin' him. Let him tell ye about it."

The officer repressed a chuckle. "Better get it straight. I'm not exactly commander of the scout company. My present command is a company of the Fifth Infantry. We've been operating against old Billy Bowlegs down south — as maybe you could guess from my jaundice tan. I came out here ahead of my men, and General Harney gave me the job of forming a company of scouts for service with the Utah expedition. Temporarily I'm in command." He laughed as he added, "I suppose the reason is that no other officer has had any experience at Indian fighting. General Harney seemed to think that I'd know how to fight Cheyennes and Sioux because I've been having a rough time with the Seminoles. At any rate I'll know enough to pick men who know the tricks. That'll keep me from showing my own ignorance."

Spencer joined in the general laugh, thinking that Marcy was playing it smart. Civilian scouts would like an officer who admitted his own lack of knowledge.

"My offer's brief," Marcy went on. "One hundred dollars a month and keep until we reach Salt Lake. No discipline. Beyond that I can't tell you a thing. I don't know who will command or how the company will be organized."

"Gov'ment plannin' to fight the Utah folks?" McGee asked.

Marcy shook his head. "No. The army is going out to police the territory until proper civil arrangements can be made. We anticipate no fighting unless it be with hostile Indians along the line of march."

Trent cut in derisively, winking at Spencer. "McGee's worried. Bein' as how he was kind of a shirttail Mormon before he got run outa the territory, he's skeered to go back for fear some of his ole wives will ketch up with him."

Marcy apparently had been briefed on the McGee background. "We'd like to have you with us, McGee," he said. "You know the country as well as anyone."

"Sounds like it ain't my cup o' doggone tea," McGee grumbled.

"Why not? Personal matters won't become involved. If you don't care to go all the way to Utah, I'd like to hire you on for a part of the trip, say through the South Pass or across the Wasatch."

McGee climbed to his feet a bit unsteadily. "Nope," he stated positively. "I'm bettin' the Utah fellers ain't goin' to like this here expeedishun. There'll be trouble. When it comes, I ain't figgerin' to be in no dad-blamed army camp."

Captain Marcy looked incredulous. "You mean you believe the Mormons will fight — and you'll expect to help them?"

"Not exactly. I figger they'll put up a scrap o' some sort — and I ain't plannin' to be in that part o' the country when it happens. Count me out and fergit ye ever talked to me about it." He wheeled with the final statement and shuffled out of the room without a backward glance.

To Spencer it seemed like a good time to declare his own disinterest, but he hated to embarrass Captain Marcy. The officer seemed like a decent sort and certainly the scouts would be needed. Two refusals in a row might make the man's job a little difficult for him.

Suddenly he thought of a way out. Callahan's remark to the English girl might well be turned to account. "Sorry I can't help you out, Captain," he said quietly, "but I'm kinda tied up in a deal with Anvil Callahan. I'd be happy to serve with a man who seems to know what he's doing, but I'll be too busy."

"Scouts company wages will be better than you could pick up driving a wagon."

"I don't plan to drive a wagon."

Marcy looked up quickly at the tone. Then he nodded, respecting the finality in it. "It's your business. Do you expect to be with the expedition, in case we might call on you in an emergency?"

"Just now I don't know."

Again Marcy did not pursue the partial answer and Spencer liked him for it. The man might have used his commission to do a lot of poking into other folks' affairs but he was restraining himself. It was something a bit unusual to find a regular army officer who was disposed to treat mountain men like human beings.

"I reckon these other men will take good care of you, Captain," Spencer said, arising. "Other trappers will be coming in from day to day. Sorry I can't oblige you." Then he followed McGee's trail to the door.

He went straight back to Callahan's shack and woke the Irishman from a noisy afternoon nap. "Wake up, you redheaded bog-trotter!" he growled, shaking an enormous shoulder. "You sound like the ice going out of the upper river."

Callahan was awake in an instant, a frown changing to a grin and then back to a frown again. "Go 'way, ye blatherskite. I'm still disgusted wid ye'."

"I'm going as soon as I tell you something. A few minutes ago I turned down a proposition to become an army scout. I told the officer that I had a deal with you that I wouldn't leave. If he comes around here, you can help the idea along. It won't be our fault if he thinks the deal is all business."

"Yer idea o' honest lyin', I suppose?" Anvil asked sourly. "Well, me bucko, I'm thinkin' I kin make a dacent citizen of ye yet. Mebbe I was thinkin' along that line when I told the lady ye was me partner. I got wagons fer Santa Fe and I got wagons goin' with the army. I need another man for wagon boss. Whichever way Donnel goes is yours. Right?"

"Thanks," Spencer said quietly. "For you that's almost human. When do I start?"

"No tellin'. Got to see how things turn out. Fer the time bein' ye kin gad about the settlement to suit yerself."

Spencer spent the afternoon roaming through the wagon camps studying the outfits and the piles of supplies and equipment. Always he had an eye cocked for Curt Donnel, but at the same time he was able to make some good guesses as to the size and nature of the proposed expedition. Without question it was going to be big. He guessed that the army was carrying supplies for an occupation period as well as for the march itself. The collection of wagons hinted at a baggage train far larger than would be needed by anything short of a major army.

By dusk he had covered the area pretty thoroughly without seeing any sign of Donnel. It worried him a little. Maybe the man had slipped away, perhaps toward Santa Fe.

Then he remembered Donnel's character and refused to accept the explanation. Donnel was too bold to be scared off easily. There was no real evidence against him on the fur deal and the man could not know yet that Dan Spencer was on his trail. Not that the latter point would have worried him too much. Spencer could not prove anything about the old Mexican affair any more that he could prove that Donnel had planned the raid of last night.

He lingered for some time over his evening meal at the Wagon Train, hoping that McGee might come in, but none of the mountain men appeared. It seemed likely that Captain Marcy had done a good job of enlisting. Spencer decided to make one quick round of the saloons in the early evening. He did not know just what he hoped to accomplish, but he would feel easier if he could find some indication that Donnel was still around Leavenworth.

For an hour he wandered in and out, nursing drinks which he never permitted himself to consume. Every place was crowded and it took a little time to make a thorough inspection, but the fact also had its advantages. He did not have to run much risk of being drawn into conversation.

Finally he found the man he was hunting. He had elbowed his way to a long bar, turning to survey the crowd before ordering anything. Instantly he caught the eye of Curt Donnel. The man was staring at him so intently that there could be no question of recognition.

Donnel's face showed something like panic for an instant. Then he turned and headed for the open door. Spencer tried to follow but only succeeded in stirring up a mild uproar among the men who objected to his unceremonious plunge. By the time he was clear of the mob around the bar he knew that pursuit was useless. Even if he had been able to catch up with Donnel, there was nothing to be gained. This was not the way to handle it.

He blamed himself mentally for the hastiness but at the same time realized that Donnel had been guilty of a greater mistake. The man's flight established one thing clearly. Donnel knew Spencer and was afraid of him. It was impossible to believe that he would connect Spencer with the intended victim of the fur raid, so the guilt had to be something of a different nature. For the first time in nine years Spencer knew that his suspicions had really been founded upon something substantial. Now if he could only find some way to make the man talk . . .

After a few minutes he moved out into the street, content to let matters stand for the night. His whole prospect was as hopeless as it had ever been, but he did not permit himelf to think about that aspect of it.

Somehow he would get to Donnel. That was a promise to himself; how he would do it was something he didn't propose to worry about just now.

He stood irresolutely outside the saloon for a few minutes, trying to decide on his next move. He knew he ought to tell Callahan of this newest development, but he didn't like the idea of depending too much on even such a good friend as Anvil. There was no point in running to him with every little thing that happened.

When he turned away toward the Wagon Train he was still not certain about his decision and the fact made him turn once as he half made up his mind to pass the word to Anvil. The move told him something which drove the other question out of his thoughts. He was being followed. A man had ducked out of sight so hurriedly that there could be no other explanation.

Instantly Spencer became a mountain man again. A man who had been trailed by skulking Indians knew what to do on such an occasion, even though surrounded by shacks instead of trees and canyons. For about ten minutes Spencer led his man a leisurely chase through dark streets and lighted ones, getting several glimpses of the pursuer. He was tall and rather slender, his dark garments making him a good bet for the job he was doing. A high-crowned, broad-brimmed hat hid his features, but the shape of the hat hinted that the fellow was a Mexican.

Donnel was behind the new development, Spencer was sure. It was a full warning that the man would prove to be no mean antagonist. Clearly he had some sort of organization which could be moved into action on short notice.

Without appearing to be suspicious, Spencer covered enough ground to make certain that only one man was behind him, then he wandered out of town to the south, noticing a light in Callahan's shack as he passed. Once away from the Irishman's corrals, he was clear of all buildings. The whispering Missouri flanked him on the left while unbroken prairie stretched away to the right. Behind him he could detect the shuffle of soft footsteps which told him that his man was maintaining the same interval.

He slowed the pace deliberately, letting the man close in. It required only a minute to learn that the fellow was not merely keeping him under surveillance. Those stealthy footsteps were coming closer, soft as ever but a little more rapid in their tempo. The pursuer was closing in for an assault.

Still Spencer did not come to a complete halt. He wanted his movements to sound unhurried, as though he had nothing on his mind but a casual stroll. The attacker was counting on surprise; maybe that very factor could be employed against him.

He turned his head as he continued to move forward, presently outlining the lithe figure of the tracker against a blur of distant lights. The man was very close now. At any moment he would have to discard his stealth and gamble on a sudden attack.

Suddenly it came. The lean man darted forward almost without a sound. Spencer met the assault as he might have met that of a lurking Sioux, one big hand darting out to intercept the knife thrust which he could not quite see. A flicker of distant light on the darting blade gave him all the clue he needed and he felt the jolt of the swinging arm as his fingers closed on a hard wrist. For an instant the attacker was thrown off balance by the unexpected resistance and Spencer took full advantage. Twisting hard at the captured hand, he swung his other fist at the tall man's face. It was the same strategy he had used against the knife wielder aboard the flatboat, but this time he did not labor under the disadvantage of being flat on his back. The vicious twist brought a quick groan of anguish, but the punch blotted out the sound almost before it could be uttered. Then the man went limp, supported only by the arm which Spencer still held.

Spencer had never considered himself a clever fighter — and he had the scars to prove it — but he was too experienced to be caught by an ancient trick. He flung himself hard at the man beneath him, hammering in another blow. There was no reaction. The attacker was not faking; he was out cold.

Retaining his grip on the man's right wrist, he groped for the fallen knife. It was a long thin-bladed weapon similar to the one he had captured on the previous evening. A long throw sent it over the bluff and into the river and then he searched his prisoner. He found nothing in the fellow's pockets, but another knife was suspended on a lanyard between the thug's shoulder blades. That followed its mate into the river.

Suddenly the man uttered a low moan and began to writhe. Spencer wasted no mercy on him. An open hand cuffed hard against the fellow's face and Spencer snapped, "Stop squirming and start to talk! Who sent you out here to knife me?"

The reply was a desperate blow at Spencer's face. He took it on the shoulder and cuffed again, twisting the imprisoned arm into a hammer lock. It rolled the prisoner to a position where he could not strike back.

"Talk fast or I'll break your arm so you won't be doing any knife work for a long time!"

The pain brought a string of whining Spanish oaths, so Spencer cuffed him again. It wasn't likely that this fellow would understand anything but force. "Talk English, and do it fast or I'll break your arm just for good measure!"

"Eet ees one beeg meestake," the man whined, surrendering quickly. "I deed not know —"

"Stop lying! You followed me long enough to know exactly what you were doing. I want to know why."

There was no answer, so Spencer heaved a little harder on the clamped arm. "Spill it or the provost will have a dead man to puzzle over tomorrow!"

There was another groan and the man howled, "I talk. I talk."

"Get at it then. Who hired you to kill me?"

"Eet ees the *Señor* Cat-lett. He promise mucho *dinero* eef you die."

"Catlett, eh? Does he always go by that name now?"

"Please, *señor*, I do not know another name. Only Catlett."

"He pointed me out to you?"

"*Si, señor*. At *la cantina* he show me."

"You work for him other times?"

"*Si, señor*. Only this morning I come in from Santa Fe weeth my wagon."

"What about the man on the other end of this Santa Fe trade? Does he call your crooked boss Catlett too?"

"*Señor*, believe me. I know only what I have tell you."

"You haven't told me a thing yet. Speak up now and let's have the whole yarn on the Santa Fe business. Who handles that end? What do you carry? I want it all, mind you, or you know what happens to you!"

The Mexican became almost frantic as a little extra pressure was applied. He practically babbled as he tried to get out the rest of his story. Boiled down, it provided Spencer with much that he needed to know. For several years Donnel had been operating in partnership with a Mexican named Garcia. Part of their trade along the Santa Fe trail was legitimate but more of it was smuggling or handling stolen goods. It seemed pretty certain that the knifing job had been just an added chore for the Mexican wagoner. He didn't know why his victim was to be killed.

Spencer thought it over for a minute or two, then yanked his prisoner to his feet. He didn't propose to kill the man, however richly that fate might be deserved, but he didn't want to have the fellow take word back to Donnel.

"Start walking," he ordered, pulling the hammer lock up so tight that the prisoner bent over as he moved. "Right out there toward the river."

"Please, *señor*. I do not sweem. Do not —"

"Good. That suits me fine. Now shut up and keep going!"

He steered his man along the low bluff until an oblong shadow in the water below indicated that a scow of some sort had been pulled up. With his free hand Spencer pulled out his gun and swung it in a short arc against the top of the Mexican's head. It was a blow calculated to knock the man out for some time to come. The fellow sagged to the ground and Spencer grimly rolled him over until he tumbled to the sand at the water's edge. After that it was the work of only a minute or two to load the unconscious man aboard the scow and shove it off into the current, first making certain that no poles or paddles were aboard. The swift currents of the Big Muddy ought to put the Mexican out of touch with his crooked employer for some time to come.

Ten minutes later Spencer was in Callahan's shack, telling his story. "So it's a cinch Donnel knows me. That puts a new light on the problem. Surprise is out of the question now — and I'll have to be on the lookout for another knifing attempt. He won't quit because his first agent failed."

Anvil Callahan had been listening with gravity, but now he let his red features twist into a broad smile. "We'll keep him guessin', Danny. Ye're gittin' outa Leavenworth right off. Come mornin' both yerself and the Mex'll be missin'. Mebbe Donnel will figger ye've killed each other."

"What's the good o' that? I can't pin the crook down if I'm not in a position to keep an eye on him."

"Trust Callahan, me bucko. I'll not let the rascal give us the slip. There's a score o' me own I've got to settle with him, ye'll remimber. Didn't he beat me outa likely customers by piratin' 'em?"

"Noble Callahan!" Spencer chuckled. "But have it your own way. Got any ideas as to where I should go?"

"A couple. One of thim we won't mention, bein' as we're frinds. The other's more to the point. I got a job fer ye."

"I might have known," Spencer growled. "One for me and two for Callahan. Do your friendly gestures always have to be mostly for your own good?"

"Don't be blackguardin' all the time, ye spalpeen! Now wait here a bit whilst I find the laddie I want ye to talk to. Callahan's goin' to git ye straightened out in spite o' yer nasty tongue."

He slipped out of the shack before Spencer could reply, leaving the younger man to smile in the dim light of the lantern. If Anvil had an idea it was probably a good one; most of Callahan's ideas were.

CHAPTER FIVE

Callahan returned so promptly that spencer knew he could have gone no farther than the warehouse or the wagon park. With him was a young fellow of perhaps nineteen, a handsome, clear-skinned youngster who was trying hard to grow a mustache.

"Here ye be, Jim," Callahan said, turning. "Take a good squint at Dan Spencer so ye'll know him when ye meet him again. I figure ye'll pick him up somewhere in the neighborhood o' the Little Kaw."

The youth nodded, somber dark eyes studying Spencer with frank boldness. "I'll be ridin' a piece with him," he said quietly. "We'll know each other right well, I guess, before I shove ahead at daylight."

"Sounds like my plans are all made for me," Spencer commented dryly. "Would it be asking too much if I wanted to know what this is all about?"

Callahan gave him a big grin, winking at his youthful companion. "This here is Jim Hickok, Danny. He'll guide ye part o' the way. Trust him fer anything; he's a smart boy."

It was a broad guarantee for Anvil Callahan to make and Spencer studied the youngster a little more carefully. He saw only an alert-looking young man in worn garments and broken-down boots, but he knew that it would not do to underestimate the boy. Callahan didn't give his approval without knowing exactly what he was doing.

"You still haven't told me what sort of deal is on the fire," he persisted.

"Ye're bossin' a train o' five wagons that I'm sendin' down the river. Jim will give ye the directions after ye git on the trail. Ye'll pick up enough flour in barrels to load the five wagons. Bring it back here."

"Sounds easy enough."

"Nothin' tough about it. Even a nacheral-born idjit like yerself kin handle it. The teamsters are harnessin' up now, so git yerself ready. Better pick yer own nag and saddle."

"Sounds like I'm being sent along just to get me out of town."

"It'll do fer that — but likewise it lets me keep Clancy here. Ye kin do me a favor by goin', and sarve yer own purpose at the same time. And I'll be lookin' after things whilst yer gone."

He swung to face the youthful guide. "Jim, will ye be afther askin' Clancy to pick a good nag or two fer Danny to choose from? He'll be along to jine ye jist as soon as I pour a few more purrls o' wisdom into his thick head. We want the whole shebang on the road inside the half hour."

The heavy brogue slid away with the Irishman's grin. He was almost grim as he turned back to Spencer. "I'm meddlin' in the Kansas troubles, Dan. Hope ye're not prejoodiced?"

"It's none of my affair — although I've had a hankering to see the free-state boys get even for some o' the raw deals they've had to swallow."

"Then ye'll like this all right. That Jim Hickok's a Jayhawker. His outfit's takin' up where old John Brown left off, only they ain't actin' quite so bold because they know the Demmycrats in Washin'ton are all on the side o' the Missouri gang. They don't raid the pro-slave settlements but they sure do annoy 'em a heap. That's how the flour comes into it. They hornswoggled a river pilot into runnin' his boat aground where the flour had to be unloaded to float the vessel. The flour belonged to this here Sons o' the South outfit but the Jayhawker boys stole it from 'em."

"You mean you're buying stolen flour?" Spencer exclaimed.

"Not exactly. The Jayhawkers owe me some money fer some guns I brung in to 'em. I'm takin' the flour fer my pay."

"How does 'Honest Anvil Callahan' square that with his reputation?"

Callahan looked aggrieved. "I'm sort of a honest bandit," he explained. "What I promise I make good on, ye know that. But I never promised nothin' to them Border Ruffians. Their loss is my gain — and mebbe the country's."

"Suppose we're picked up with it?"

"The Jayhawkers will be guardin' ye — out o' sight. Anyway, they've re-marked the barrels."

Spencer stood up, a half smile quirking his lips. "I'm meeting a new Callahan," he said slowly, "but I think I understand — and sympathize. Maybe it's time the Missouri bully-boys got a dose of their own medicine."

It was close to midnight when the five wagons rolled out to the south, Spencer riding ahead with the young guide. No one said anything until they were well clear of town and then Spencer suggested, "Better give me the whole layout, Jim. How far is it and when will your boys pick us up?"

"Call me Bill," the youth requested. "James Butler Hickok's a mite fancy for this country. Most o' the outfit call me Bill and I like it fine."

"Suits me. Now let's hear the yarn."

"We'll bear west a spell to get around a couple o' towns where the Missourians are strong. Then we move south toward Lawrence. That's where the flour is hidden. Three days easy travel, I make it." Then he added, "If we don't get jumped."

"Then the flour is not along the Missouri?"

"Nope. On the Kansas. That makes it easier, I reckon."

"Likely."

"You'll have to remember your trail because you'll be alone coming back. It'll be better for you if none of our outfit shows with you."

"Sounds reasonable."

"But we'll have riders close. If trouble starts you can expect plenty of help."

Under other circumstances Spencer might have been amused at the youngster's calm confidence, but somehow it was not easy to take him lightly. The boy was playing a man's part in a pretty deadly game —

and evidently playing it so well that others were relying on him for important work. In the next couple of hours Spencer learned a number of significant items about the smouldering civil war in Kansas. Among other things, he discovered that there was a strong antagonism to the Utah expedition. The free-staters insisted that the whole affair was just a blind on the part of the pro-slavery interests in the administration, a device to take popular attention from the unjust way in which decent citizens were being treated in Kansas.

A good hour before dawn, Hickok spurred ahead after a few parting bits of advice on the route to be followed and then Spencer was on his own. By that time he had forgotten his first objections to the project. He was even a little sorry that he couldn't do something more definite in the way of helping the Kansans.

At dawn he called a halt, giving the oxen a long rest while the men enjoyed a good breakfast and an hour of lounging in the early sunshine. Two of the drivers he had known before, a couple of hardy bullwhackers named Jonas and McCready. The other three answered to the names of Rusty, Duke and O'Rourke. None of them talked very much, but it was satisfyingly clear that they were Callahan's regulars and nothing else mattered.

They made twelve miles that day, camping early after the day and night haul. Twice passing riders had hailed them and once they'd seen a wagon at a distance, but there was no sign of trouble.

At dusk on the second day, Hickok appeared once more, announcing that the entire area was clear of enemies. Evidently the Missouri men had given up their pirated flour as a dead loss. That suited Spencer well enough. He didn't mind the thought of a fight but he didn't want to take freight back to Leavenworth in front of pursuers whose claim would undoubtedly be legal.

He might have spared himself the worry. As usual, Callahan had known exactly what he was doing. So did the men who made up the Jayhawker band. The wagons were halted shortly after noon of the third day, remaining idle in a secluded swale until dark. Then Hickok led them on to a sod house where a half dozen horses were tethered. Silent men mounted to join them and soon they were all busy with the work of loading flour barrels into the big prairie schooners. Within the hour they were on the move again and by dawn were back at the spot where they had spent the previous afternoon.

After that it was ridiculously easy, even though the month of June came in on the wings of a driving rainstorm that bogged the loaded wagons and kept them idle for two days. The waiting and the subsequent slow pace gave Spencer plenty of chance to think. Partly he considered the odd tangle of political affairs which was blending the Kansas struggle with this projected expedition to Utah, but mostly he thought about his own problems.

One idea kept coming back to him. The Mexican knifeman had mentioned someone by the name of

Garcia as being Donnel's partner. Garcia was a common enough name in Mexico, but there was a good chance that something more than mere coincidence was indicated. There had been a guerrilla chief named Garcia along the border during the Mexican War. There had even been a report that it was Garcia who had gotten control of a mysteriously lost wagon train. A young cavalry lieutenant named Spencer had resigned his commission under a cloud as a result of the loss — and a freighter named Donnel had been right on the spot at the time. It sounded like a real lead.

The train was approaching Leavenworth when Callahan rode out to meet it. He exchanged brief comments with Spencer and gave his orders. "Swing a mite to the left. We'll head around the town and into the army camp. I'll show ye the place meself."

"What place?"

"The Callahan camp, no less. I been makin' me a deal with the army, me bucko. Sold 'em the flour jist as she rides — and hired out the wagons to haul it west. We'll line up with the other wagons I've got into the deal and thin no dirty Missouri scum will dare to lay claim to it."

Spencer smiled thinly at the uncomplimentary reference to the real owners of the load, but his question ignored it. "You expecting me to ride this train?"

"Suit yerself. There's always Matt Clancy — but yer man Donnel is goin' along, so I thought ye'd be likin' the chore."

"What do you know about Donnel?"

"A fair bit. Didn't I promise I'd kape an eye on the blackguard? He's got a train of a dozen wagons, pullin' most of 'em off'n his Santa Fe run. Loaded with army gear and waitin' right now fer the order to move."

"When will that be?"

Callahan's big shoulders hunched helplessly. "They started gatherin' this army last March, sayin' as how they'd hit fer Utah as soon as the mud settled. Right now it looks like the gov'mint can't make up its mind whether it wants the troops in Utah or right here to look after these Kansas elections that're comin' up."

They rolled into the outskirts of the huge camp and Spencer could see that the week of absence had made quite a difference in the place. More wagons had crowded in; more men bustled about. Once more he knew that feeling of mingled nostalgia and resentment as he studied the arrangement of freight wagons and troop quarters. Likely he'd never quite get over the feeling. A line or a square of those big blue Conestogas with the sway-backed ozenbrig tops always suggested something to him — and not all of the suggestion was distasteful. Once he had taken some pride seeing such wagons properly organized.

Spencer noted that no cavalry appeared in camp. At least six companies of infantry were on hand, even though most of the immediate scene was the wagon camp. Army wagons were parked in double rows back to back for easier hitch-ups, their alignment distinguishing them from the trains of the independent contractors, who seemed to prefer the trail-tested rectangle. With the Cheyennes still on the warpath there would probably be plenty of opportunity for that defensive formation to prove its value, Spencer decided.

"Where's Donnel's outfit?" Spencer asked as he watched his teamsters wheel into position before spanning out. Callahan's wagoners knew their business, all right. The only wagon boss they needed was one who could keep out of their way and let them handle their duties.

"Mebbe a mile closer to the fort and near the river. He's keepin' kinda clear o' the other outfits."

"Does he know about his Mex thug or me?"

"Not as I've heard of. Looks like he's still kinda puzzled."

"Good. Heard any more from McGee?"

"Nothin' only he drew some money and claimed he was lightin' a shuck fer the west. I didn't ask no questions."

Next morning Spencer walked slowly through the big, sprawling encampment studying the number and types of vehicles being gathered for the long haul across the Rockies. Gradually he worked clear of the more congested areas and presently entered what he guessed would be the camp of the newly formed scout company.

Cal Trent was on hand, his gray beard as unkempt as usual, and he hastened to pass on a message from Mormon McGee. "Mormon says to tell ye he's movin' on to the Pacific," the old trapper reported. "That's the only place left where a man don't have to take sides in no doggone fights."

"Looks mighty peaceful around here," Spencer observed.

Trent chuckled a bit scornfully. "Never seen such dadratted foolishness in all my born days. This here army ain't showin' no signs o' movin'. Most o' the freight outfits is ready to go, but there ain't nobody to order 'em out. The troops ain't ready and the officers don't seem to do nothin' but run around tryin' to look important."

"I wonder if somebody is trying to have the whole thing called off?"

Trent shot him a quizzical glance. "Could be," he said dryly. "There's some as thinks it should be."

When Spencer did not comment further, Trent asked, "Did Cap Marcy hit ye up again to jine us?"

"No. Why do you ask?"

"He's interested. A couple o' times he axed me about ye. Wasn't much I could tell him, bein' as how ye've been mostly a Missouri River man with yer pelts while I've hauled mine to Santy Fee most every spring."

"That reminds me," Spencer said quickly. "Do you know a freighter in Santa Fe named Garcia?"

Trent dug gnarled fingers into the gray beard, scratching vigorously as though to stimulate thought. "No real freighter, I reckon. There's a Jose Garcia operates around that part o' the country, but he's more of a smuggler than a freighter."

"Sounds like the man. Was he a guerrilla in the war?"

"Like enough. Lots of 'em was. All of 'em got pardons when we took over the territory. That made 'em honest men, ready to set up in smugglin' and gun-runnin' to the Injuns."

"Thanks. I'll remember that."

"Happens we'll be hittin' the trail right soon now," Trent stated, changing the subject abruptly. "Then Mormons that was back east tryin' to smooth things over is on the way home. Got into Leavenworth yestiday. Kinda bad timin' on their part, I'd figger. They hit town about two hours after the word got around about the Handcart Brigade."

"Better chew that up in smaller bites," Spencer said. "I lost you after the first swallow."

It took some time and questioning, but eventually Trent managed to make the picture clear. During the previous spring and summer an unusually large number of Mormon converts had gathered along the Missouri for the trip west. Many of them had come from the British Isles, lured by the persuasiveness of the Mormon missionaries who were operating in the English factory towns. Apparently the Mormon transport organization was not nearly as efficient as the missionary department, for no supplies had been provided for the emigrants.

Wagons and provisions were gathered in insufficient quantity and after a series of delays the last detachment started west along the Overland Trail with their scanty belongings loaded into pushcarts. There had been grim jokes about the Handcart Brigade or Pushcart Army, as they were variously called, and men of judgment had predicted disaster. The best-equipped trains found trouble in making the trip. Nothing but tragedy could be expected for greenhorns sent out afoot at least two months after properly equipped trains should have departed.

"The wust happened," Trent affirmed. "Some o' the early outfits managed to git through to Salt Lake more dead than alive, but the last batch got snowed in near Black's Fork. Buried 'em at Fort Bridger this spring when the snow went out."

"And the Mormons didn't try to rescue them?"

"Seems like they didn't. Folks around here is some riled up about it. There was a mite o' trouble when them Mormon fellers got off'n a steamboat yestiday. Provost had to put a guard around their hotel to keep the mob from bustin' 'em up."

Spencer could understand that too. The people of Leavenworth had been divided in their attitude toward the Utah expedition, but this report would turn them against the Mormons. The Handcart Brigade had included a large number of women. Frontier folks would hold it against the Mormons that the tragedy had been allowed to happen.

"Anyway, we'll be movin' now," Cal Trent growled. "Peace talks have plumb busted wide open and the Mormon fellers are headed home. That means we ain't got no more excuse to set around on our tails and wait."

Spencer was on his way out of the camp when he was intercepted by a tall officer who stepped out of the only decent-looking tent in sight. Captain Marcy still wore his pleasant smile, but Spencer felt a moment of uneasiness. Trent had hinted that Marcy still wanted him.

“Didn’t change your mind, did you, Spencer?” Marcy asked abruptly.

The younger man shook his head. “No. Just dropped in to visit Trent.”

“Sorry. I’d hoped otherwise. Anyway, I’d like to talk to you a minute. Do you mind?”

“No reason to. What do you want to talk about?”

“You.”

“What about me?” He knew that he didn’t need to ask the question. A hint of embarrassment in Marcy’s face told him what was coming.

“I’ll be blunt,” the captain stated. “I have come to the conclusion that you are the Lieutenant Daniel Spencer who was with Doniphan’s dragoons in the Mexican War. I’ve spent some time and effort getting the facts and I believe I have them straight. You were cashiered over the business of losing a supply train to the enemy. You fought the charge but couldn’t prove your innocence. Apparently no one else could prove anything, but you resigned, declaring that you proposed to clear yourself. Did you ever succeed?”

“Isn’t the army record clear on that point?” There was bitterness in the tone in spite of Spencer’s effort to make his voice calm.

“I found no record. However, I’m not making this an official investigation. My men told me that you know the South Pass better than any of them and I wanted to get you into the scout company. Trent hinted that you were sore at the army and I had hopes that we could straighten out your personal feeling and keep this on a friendly basis. I have done a lot of snooping into your personal history, but I am keeping it entirely to myself."

"Thanks. But you have wasted your time. I still think the army handed me a raw deal but I can't prove a thing. While that is the situation, I don't propose to deal with the military."

"I'm sorry," Marcy told him. "I had hoped we might do something about it. We'll need someone like you before this job is done."

"Thanks," Spencer said again. "I'd like it fine to serve under a man like you but —"

"It's your choice. If I can do anything, let me know. I've come to the conclusion that you were in the right."

"Decent of you to say that, Captain. Somehow it helps. I'll be going."

He hurried from the scout camp, not trusting himself to speak further. A fellow could weaken pretty easily when he was dealing with a man like Marcy. It wasn't safe to stand around and talk; too many things had to be done.

Which was a reminder in itself. He wasn't doing a thing about the business of getting a line on Curt Donnel — and the expedition might move out at any moment.

CHAPTER SIX

It was dusk when spencer returned to the Callahan camp and by that time he had managed to shake off some of the gloom which had settled upon him after his talk with Captain Marcy. It was too bad that he could not do a favor for a man who wanted to be his friend, but his own problem had to come first. After nine years of fruitless searching, he was on a hot trail, a trail which had to be followed.

When supper was over he slipped away quietly, working toward the river in a search for the Donnel outfit. He found it set apart from the other wagon divisions. A line of brush served to make the Donnel camp quite private, but it also offered an observation post for Spencer, a rather important point for a man who needed to memorize the faces of the enemy.

The Donnel wagons now numbered fourteen; they were spanned out in a long rectangle, six on each side and two at the far end. Near the open end men lounged about a fire and Spencer could make out the heavy features of his old enemy. Donnel was keeping himself smoothly shaven nowadays.

An hour's study of the camp told him little. The men did not move around very much and when they did it was to perform small camp chores, always at the same end of the rectangle. Spencer was reminded of Callahan's opinion that Donnel was keeping remarkably quiet about something. Did it have to do with the fact that his crew seemed to avoid the closed end of the formation?

Presently the drivers began to roll up in their blankets and soon the camp was asleep except for Donnel himself and two men who had hunkered down by the dying fire. First trick guards, Spencer thought, deciding that he might as well give up and get some sleep.

Then Donnel muttered something to the guards and walked slowly away toward the closed end of the camp. Something in his manner hinted at purpose, so Spencer moved with him, angling toward the same spot. By keeping low he could see his man's legs beneath the line of wagons, losing him only when Donnel reached the far end. Apparently he had climbed to the seat of one of the two Conestogas which closed in the narrow end of the rectangle.

Spencer moved in with all the stealth acquired by long experience in the mountains and was quickly rewarded by a mutter of voices. Someone else was in there, someone who had not appeared at the fire.

Twice he caught the rumble of Donnel's heavy bass, but only when he was within a dozen feet did he hear a reply. Then he picked up a sound which made him blink. There was no mistaking that cool English accent. The English girl was Donnel's secret. Apparently she had found someone to handle her case.

Almost at the same moment he knew that she was angry. "I must ask you to leave at once," she said sharply. "I'll not tolerate either you or your proposals!"

"Don't git high and mighty with me, lady," Donnel growled. "Out in this country a woman ain't got no call to put on airs."

"Go away or I'll —"

"Yuh'll what?" The hoarse laugh was derisive. "Make a squawk and yuh'll have the provost down on us. Wouldn't that be jest fine!"

"I said go away! I won't have you talking to me like that even if calling for help means ruin to my plans."

"Yuh're not playin' it smart," Donnel told her, wheedling a little now. "Here we go to all this trouble to keep yuh hid — and yuh don't even appreciate the favor."

"I'm paying you well for —" She broke off with a smothered cry as a sound of scuffling issued from the wagon. Spencer jumped toward the front of the vehicle, reaching out in the darkness to find the opening in the canvas top. A flailing foot struck his groping hand and he grabbed it promptly, taking a second hold on a corduroy-clad leg. There was a startled oath and then Spencer heaved hard.

Donnel's curses rose angrily as he was hauled out of the wagon, but he seemed to think that one of his own crew was interfering. Spencer gave him no opportunity to learn differently. For years he had owed Curt Donnel a good beating and this was a fine chance. He hammered the man unmercifully, taking a few jarring blows in return but ignoring them completely. He simply shrugged them off and bored in, exultant that for once he was in a position to do some of the attacking. It was not much of a pay-off to give a man who had sent a thug to murder him, but it was better than so much of that infernal waiting and watching.

Once he slipped, almost falling as his foot found a treacherous hummock, but he recovered as Donnel tried to counterattack. The freighter was trying to get into close quarters, but Spencer fought him off with driving fists, finally landing a pair of solid blows that sent Donnel to the earth with a grunt that became almost a wheeze. Only then did Spencer think about the girl in the wagon and become alert to the actions of the two men at the fire. Both of them were staring into the darkness, trying to see what was happening there.

One of them yelled a question, but by that time Spencer had both his breath and his wits back. He made his voice purposely hoarse, calling, "Stay outa this, damn yuh!" Evidently that was the sort of answer they expected from Curt Donnel, for the pair hunkered down again and ignored the closed end of the encampment.

He turned back toward the wagon, asking quietly, "Are you all right in there, ma'am?"

"Thank you, yes. What did you do to that man?"

"Little enough. You sure he didn't hurt you any?"

"I'm quite all right. Who are you and why did you come to my assistance?"

"Never mind that part. Just believe me that it was a real pleasure. When he wakes up, tell him I'll use a gun on him the next time he tries to get smart. Meanwhile, keep a good stout club handy."

Her expression of amazement died away as he faded back into the night, pleased with himself for the first time in weeks. Getting a good crack at Curt Donnel had been an unexpected pleasure. Helping a pretty girl at the same time was just extra. It helped a man's morale.

He watched from the screen of brush until Donnel recovered his senses and went limping back to the fire. An argument ensued for some minutes, but then Donnel disappeared into tarp-enclosed space under one of the wagons. Evidently this was his regular sleeping quarters, for he did not come out again, and Spencer soon slipped away to his own camp. Several times he chuckled as he walked, wondering what Donnel was thinking. It was a shame that the old crook couldn't know who had hit him, but it was better that he ache in bewilderment.

Next morning he went into Leavenworth, figuring that the day would be a good one for catching up on a few odd chores. There should be little chance of stumbling on Curt Donnel since it seemed likely that the man would be resting and nursing his bruises. Spencer knew that sooner or later he would have to let his enemy know that he was alive, but it seemed like a good idea to keep him in the dark as long as possible.

The town seemed normal enough, but he was not long in spotting the infantrymen who were posted at the front of the Overland House. The army was going out of its way to protect the representatives of the territory it was getting ready to invade.

He was still studying the place when a familiar figure emerged from the hotel. The gray bonnet concealed the woman's face, but he knew no doubt as to her identity. Probably the English girl had heard some talk of the Mormon emissaries being in town and she was trying to change her plans. After last night's experience, he could not blame her.

She hesitated briefly but then started across the town to the south. That was an odd sort of move, Spencer thought; if she had risked coming out into the open she should certainly get under cover again as quickly as possible. Because he was curious — and also because he had a growing interest in the blonde woman — he followed her at a safe distance. At the same time he watched to see that no one else was trailing her.

To his surprise she went straight to Anvil Callahan's headquarters, entering the shack only long enough to learn that Callahan was not present. When she came out again Spencer was within recognition distance and she spoke to him at once. "You're Mr. Callahan's associate, aren't you?"

"That's a mighty fancy way of putting it," he countered. "But is there anything I can do for you?"

"I do not know. You remember my problem?"

"Of course."

She frowned a little, as though not quite knowing how to take that very firm assurance. "I have been — well, in hiding, waiting for a wagon train to move. Last evening I had some trouble with the man who agreed to see that I got to Utah. I was quite inclined then to break my contract with him, but this morning the choice was made for me. An army officer inspected the wagons and ordered me out."

Spencer looked his astonishment. "First I've heard of any inspections. Mostly none of the officials seems to know or care what's in any of the wagons. Do you suppose your — er, friend — took this means of taking out his spite on you?"

She met his glance squarely. "What makes you think he might have felt spiteful? I simply said we had trouble."

"I just jumped at conclusions." Spencer tried to cover the mistake he had made. "A pretty woman is dependent upon a man who hasn't any manners or social training. It's easy to guess what must have happened."

He could see the change in her expression as she listened. Suddenly she smiled. "Now I understand," she told him. "That bruise on your cheek isn't very old. It might have happened last night — to a man who had a voice like yours. I think maybe you should do some of the explaining instead of asking me to do it all."

"Maybe we should step into Anvil's shack," he suggested. "This could turn out to be quite a consultation and we'd both be better off if we were not out in the open for the wrong folks to see us."

She turned without a word and went back into the shanty. Spencer seized the opportunity to ask the next question. "Want to tell me why you visited the Mormons this morning?"

"The obvious reason. I'm looking for help again."

"Did you get any?"

"Only an idea. They can't do anything for me, in fact they tried to dissuade me. However, they did mention that it is rumored that some women will be carried along in army wagons when the train moves. Their suggestion was that Mr. Callahan might find a way to get me into that part of the train."

"Sounds like something Callahan would get some fun out of doing," Spencer admitted. "I hadn't even heard about it."

"May I ask how you happened to be on hand last evening? I haven't thanked you —"

"No thanks due," he interrupted hastily. "I just happened to be looking after a bit of my own business. Your friend Donnel — or Catlett, if that is what he's calling himself now — is an old enemy of mine who needs watching. It was just my good luck that I had a good excuse to wallop him a couple of times."

She was studying him strangely now. "Memory is a peculiar sort of thing, isn't it?" she mused. "When I began to connect your voice with the voice of the man who aided me last night, I seemed to call up several other memories. Now I know why Catlett's voice always seemed oddly familiar — and that tells me who you are. Once you wore whiskers and refused to guide me to Utah. Catlett was the false buyer who sent his thugs to steal your furs!"

"Ma'am, your memory is sure remarkable," he assured her solemnly.

"Mostly I remember how you smelled on that boat." She laughed. "You were well disguised after you had bathed."

"I reckon I musta been sorta ripe," he admitted, drawling it out to cover his surprise at her show of humor. The girl had been so intense about everything that he had not expected her to laugh over such a matter.

Anvil Callahan came in at that point and Spencer glared his disapproval of the bad timing. Another ten minutes and this interview might have worked itself to a pleasant level. "The lady's giving us another chance, Anvil," he announced. "Sounds to me like your kind of a job this time. Just crooked enough to appeal to you and safe enough to keep your big carcass out of any personal trouble."

"Listen to the tongue of him!" Callahan glowered. "Shet yer sassy face and let the lady tell her story."

She repeated what she had told Spencer. When it was complete, Callahan nodded sagely. "Could happen they got a good idee," he agreed. "They's wimmen goin', I know that. But it won't be aisy to put in somebody what's not army folks."

"May I tell you my story?" she asked quietly. "You must understand how important this is to me."

"I been a mite curious," Callahan admitted, glancing at Spencer.

"You have heard of the Handcart Brigade?"

"Where's the man who ain't heard tell of 'em?"

"My sister was a member of that group. I must know what happened to her. That is the main reason why I visited those Mormon officials today. They were polite enough, but they didn't know anything. I must know whether she survived or whether she was one of those poor souls who died in the mountain winter."

"Why not wait here until the news comes through?" Spencer cut in. "Before long there ought to be a complete report."

"I must know for myself — and again I think I might as well go into detail. You see I'm depending on your interest. I want you to understand my feeling because I hope that will make you willing to help me. Will you listen to an explanation that is so frankly selfish?"

"I'm like Callahan," Spencer told her. "I been a mite curious."

The girl's smile was fleeting. "My sister Anne was a peculiar sort of girl. She had not lived at home for a number of years, insisting that our rather comfortable family life was unbearable for her when poorer folk had to exist in poverty. She went to live in a slum, calling upon us only when she wanted funds for her welfare work. She was an idealist, a humanitarian — and an impractical dreamer. People took advantage of her at every opportunity, but for every shattered delusion she managed to develop a few new ones. Adopting Mormonism was the crowning touch.

"We did not hear from her for several months and then we learned that she had sailed for America with a number of other people who had been persuaded to give up English factory towns for the promises of Utah. She wrote us from Philadelphia saying that she was leaving immediately for the west."

"Is there a reason why you fear she might have been in the group that was lost in the mountains?" Spencer asked.

"A very good reason. Her letter was dated July second, eighteen hundred fifty-six."

"I understand," Spencer said quietly, figuring the time quickly. Anyone who had been in Philadelphia in early July could not possibly have left the Missouri River before August, even allowing for the new railroad lines and the improved steamboat service. The girl called Anne must have been one of the last to depart for Utah, one of the party that never reached Fort Bridger alive.

"Ye'll be wantin' to take her back home?" Callahan inquired, partly to get around the uncomfortable silence.

She shook her head. "I have no home now. Perhaps I never had much of a home after my mother died. Father's attention to his business was part of the reason Anne left us — and her emigration was a sort of final blow to the grief he had been covering. He died last November. Before he died I promised him that I would find Anne and see to it that she shared the estate he was leaving to me. I think you can see now why I mean to reach Utah no matter what obstacles are placed in my way."

Callahan's bald head nodded slowly back and forth. "What kind of outfit did ye have with this Catlett-Donnel polecat?"

"Two freight wagons and twenty-two oxen. Why?"

"What marks on the beef?"

"Marks?" she asked, puzzled.

"Sure. Brands. Earmarks? Where'd ye git 'em?"

"I bought them from a dealer named Applegate. Josiah Applegate, I think it was."

"Good enough." Callahan was all business now. "Danny, me b'y, hustle over to Applegate's corrals and find out what brands thim beasts carried. Thin git the lady's stock outa that rinnygade's camp. Harness 'em up to the wagons and sind 'em here. Meanwhile I'll be lookin' into the other matter." He hesitated a moment before adding, "Ye could sind Matt Clancy to git the outfits if ye want to keep Donnel still in the dark."

"Maybe it's time I declared myself," Spencer told him quietly. "If I make him mad enough he might try a trick or two. Sooner or later I've got to smoke him out so it might as well be sooner."

"Take enough o' the b'ys wid ye," Callahan warned. "If ye're planin' to be the bait in the trap ye want to make sure it's set."

The girl stopped him as he headed for the door. "Forgive me," she said simply. "I think I must have sounded very impolite when you refused my offer that night along the river. Now I am both grateful and remorseful at the way I've sounded."

"You made just one mistake, miss," Spencer said. "You should have made your bid in daylight. It was wasting good ammunition to come around in the dark."

Then he was out of the door, more than a little pleased that he had drawn a blush. The English girl was worth a little attention. Maybe it wasn't too late to atone for his earlier neglect.

CHAPTER SEVEN

The dusty heat of midday was still sending up shimmers of discomfort when Spencer led four well-armed riders into the Donnel camp. He had told them only enough of the story to make them understand that there might be trouble, but for Callahan drivers that had been enough. They backed him grimly, studying the Donnel men who stood up to stare at them.

Curt Donnel was doing most of the staring. At sight of Spencer he turned pale, then an angry red. Once his big hand swept toward the front of his coat, but it halted there when Spencer made a similar move. It was a tipoff and Spencer kept it in mind.

"We're here for the lady's stock and wagons, Donnel," Spencer told him abruptly, not bothering to use the name that seemed to be currently in vogue. "Do you want to help cut them out or shall we do it?"

The tone was a challenge in itself and for a moment it seemed that the burly freighter would show fight. Then he glanced at the four alert men who had fanned out behind Spencer, and capitulated. Motioning toward the river, he growled, "Out there along the bank. Pick 'em yerself if yuh're so dam' smart!" Spencer was pleased to note the man's black eye.

"Nobody has to be smart to spot the Applegate brand. Sure you don't want to check and see that we don't take any of yours?"

Suddenly Donnel seemed to make up his mind. He put on a broad smile and made an elaborate bow. "I trust you, my friend. Go right ahead with your roundup. Let me know if you need help."

"Thanks. We'll get along."

"I'm sure of it, my friend. By the way, is my late passenger an old friend of yours?"

Spencer grinned. Donnel was being nastily polite in his endeavor to learn something. "Very recent," he said. "Mostly since last evening."

That took some of the smirk from the battered features. The one good eye glared malevolently and Spencer twisted the dirk a little more. "Very pleasant way to get acquainted. I liked it a lot." He motioned his men toward the river, pausing only to add, "I might as well tell you that I'm camped with Callahan's outfit. It'll save you the trouble of having me followed, in case you want to send any more of your thugs after me."

He dropped his hand to his gun as Donnel let anger get the better of him. "Careful, Curt. I don't want to shoot you yet. But I will!"

Both sides waited in silence to see what would happen. Then Donnel backed down, muttering angrily as he turned away. Spencer watched him grimly as he gestured toward the Donnel crew. "If any of you boys get ambitious to earn a little of the boss's money, just remember what happened to Schlagel and the big Mex. So long now."

A busy half hour followed, the two crews keeping clear of each other without either side relaxing for a moment. Then the girl's wagons were hauled away toward Leavenworth, McCready handling one and Jonas the other. Spencer and the other two men rode straight back to the wagon camp, leading their extra horses. Donnel was not in sight when they left.

That evening Spencer took the wagoners more completely into his confidence. While Matt Clancy still attended to routine matters of the regular trade, Spencer was accepted as temporary wagon boss, so he felt it his duty to remain at the camp. That involved some danger to the other men and he explained the situation, then organized a guard detail for the hours of darkness. The men were willing enough. Having no duties of any consequence by day, they did not object to doing a guard shift at night. Moreover, most of them were delighted at the way Spencer had rawhided Curt Donnel and were anxious to take a hand in the fun.

A couple of days of complete inactivity followed and the men began to lose some of their zest, going back to the old routine of cussing the army for its delays. June was passing and there was no sign of a movement. Men were beginning to compare this expedition with that of the unfortunate Mormon converts. Disaster had overtaken the Handcart Brigade largely because they had started west too late. Apparently the army commanders were not learning anything from past experiences of others.

Then Callahan appeared at the camp with the blonde girl's wagons, a pair of his regular drivers handling the wagons while a third man herded the spare oxen. Anvil's red face was as solemn as he could make it when he nodded a curt greeting to Spencer. "Two more wagons fer the train," he announced. "Army loads, all accordin' to contract. Here's the bills o' ladin'."

Spencer glanced at the papers and saw that they were in the name of R. E. Corliss with Callahan as agent. The lading was given as spare harness and had been checked by an officer of the quartermaster's department.

"All in order," Spencer agreed. "What about the girl?"

"That's fixed too. She's army baggage now."

"Meaning what?"

Callahan winked broadly. "Happens there's army wives wants to make sure their menfolks don't git gay with none o' them spare wives the Mormons have got. Army takes care of its own, ye know. Seems like there's wagons on the manifests that none o' the officers are likely to check."

"Who did you blackmail to get her in?"

"Always the blatherskite!" Callahan sighed. "Don't be askin' fool questions. The Callahan has his ways o' doin' things."

"By the way, is her name Corliss? I see it's here on the papers."

"Gittin' smart, ain't ye? Corliss, it is. Now don't be huntin' her up jest because ye got around to seein' that she's a rare colleen. Ye could spoil me game complete."

"Don't worry. I've got enough on my mind right now."

"Donnel?"

"Sure. Sooner or later he'll have a try at me."

"I'm countin' on it. If he gits ye I'll kape yer money what I've got on deposit."

"If he gets me you can have it."

"Ye're me b'y, Danny. It's waitin' fer the glad day I'll be." His tone changed and the brogue dropped away as he added, "I'll be havin' another lot o' wagons in a day or so. Matt will take over then. Keep yerself clear 'til then; after that ye'll be free to look after yerself any way ye want."

"Fine. Now if you'll tell me how to do it I'll be much obliged. So far I'm sticking myself up as a target and I don't know how I'll counterattack if the opportunity ever comes. Donnel seems to hold all the cards."

"It's yer own problem, Danny. There I can't help a bit."

Callahan was as good as his word. The train was completed two days later and the garrulous Clancy took charge of the camp. It left Spencer free to work on his own plans, but he couldn't seem to hit on any program that sounded even fair. Always he was in danger of being murdered — and there was absolutely nothing he could do about it.

During the rest of the month Spencer became a wanderer, scouting the Donnel camp on occasion but mostly keeping away from the Callahan outfit. So far as he could tell Curt Donnel had made no offensive move — and that worried him more than an attack. Donnel knew what he was doing; if he was waiting he probably had a good reason for it.

Once Spencer sought out Cal Trent in hopes that the scout might know something of the army's plans. It was now beginning to appear that Donnel might travel with the expedition and Spencer wanted to know what to expect. He found that the scouts had gone Indian hunting with a company of the Fifth Infantry. A band of Cheyennes had swooped down on a trail herd being moved across Kansas for the use of the army, and soldiers had been sent to recover the stolen beef. Since there were still no dragoons with the army, due to General Harney's interest in policing Kansas, infantrymen had been hastily mounted and sent out with the scout company. Not that anyone seemed to hold out much chance for their success. Regular cavalry had been skirmishing with the belligerent Cheyennes for nearly two years, invariably being out-maneuvered by the wily savages, so it wasn't expected that mounted infantry would fare any better.

Callahan summed it up pretty well. "It's a foine start the army will be gittin' — if they iver git one. Two years we been a-fightin' them heathens and the gov'mint don't even know they're on the warpath. No guards with the trail herd. No dragoons to chase 'em. Now I suppose the whole lousy army will set on its tail and wait fer more beef."

"How does your contract read?" Spencer asked dryly.

Callahan chuckled. "I ain't losin' nothin'. We git paid no matter if we're waitin' here or rollin' west. But I never had me no likin' fer so much blunderin' around."

June slid away with no change in the dreary picture, either for Spencer or for the army. Every day was the same old story of wait, eat dust, and fret over what was likely to happen. Men could not forget what had happened to the Handcart Brigade. They saw themselves being pushed into an equally dangerous position and they resented it. Not having any chance to take out their anger on the leaders responsible, they fought each other over nothing.

Then McCready caught up with Spencer one morning. "Anvil's huntin' yuh, Dan," McCready announced abruptly. "Clancy's got a stove-up laig. Mule kicked him and busted her clean through."

"I'll see him right away," Spencer agreed. The news did not come as any great shock, even though he had entertained no apprehensions about Matt Clancy. For days he had been feeling that he would travel with the Callahan outfit. Maybe it was just as well.

He spent the afternoon getting the business details straightened out and soothing the worried Callahan and that evening took over his command.

There was no sign of any trouble from Donnel or his men and after a couple of days Spencer ventured to set up an organization which would continue to operate after the train moved west. He now had eighteen wagons under his command and twenty-three men available for a share of night guard. Even if the army failed to provide troops on guard duty the Callahan wagons would be watched with care. Spencer had a very personal stake in that particular detail.

He put his program into operation so that the men would become accustomed to it, making sure that he carried a good share of the responsibility himself. During the next few months he might have to depend on the men of this wagon division and he wanted them to feel that he was really one of them.

Meanwhile, the rumors of a movement were flying thick and fast. General Harney and the missing dragoons were reported nearby. A new beef herd was supposed to be moving west ahead of the army. Orders were reputed to be ready for a march on the last day of June. Spencer ignored them all, keeping his mind on two matters only: an efficient organization of his wagon division and a careful alertness against ambush.

When June passed without any of the rumors proving true, grumbling among the teamsters increased. Every man realized that the travel season was being lost by stupidity on the part of the command. Contractors began to have trouble keeping men in camp. Mule skinners and bullwhackers who had no scruples against taking pay for a long loaf still preferred to pick up other employment. They had no desire to draw two months' easy wages in return for what they could guess was ahead of them.

Then a new lot of rumors began to go the rounds, this time backed by the sight of high-ranking officers inspecting the camp and equipment. Couriers and messengers seemed to be riding in and out of the fort at all hours and there was a last-minute check of wagon manifests. Spencer noted that all of the details were being carried out by men of the Fifth Infantry. The companies of the Tenth which had been ordered to the expedition had not yet appeared. Nor had any dragoons reported at Leavenworth. Apparently the army was going to do the job the hard way again, sending out an immense baggage train with no cavalry protection at all. This in spite of the known fact that the Cheyennes were still openly hostile.

By that time most men were too disgusted to complain. For the first time there were real signs of movement. That was an improvement; the rest could be ignored.

CHAPTER EIGHT

Another ten days of dreary waiting slipped by before the scout company with their weary infantry comrades returned to the post. Spencer heard the story from Cal Trent and it was not an encouraging one. No one had even seen an Indian. The only beef recovered had been some weak animals left behind by the raiding Cheyennes. The scouts had been too busy playing nursemaids to a lot of saddle-sore foot-sloggers to have any time for chasing redskins. To add to their disgust, the mountain men had returned to find a change of orders for Captain Marcy. The leader they had come to trust was being sent back to his regular infantry company, his place to be taken by an untried lieutenant who knew nothing of plains Indians.

"Feller name of Bickford," Trent grumbled. "Likely we'll have to put a tether on him so he won't git lost."

The time for complaints was past, however. The next day — July seventeenth — marching orders were issued. The scout company was to lead off, followed by the worn-out companies of the Fifth. Other infantry units would be spaced among the wagon trains.

Trent came to tell Spencer. "See ye tonight," he added with a grim wink. "We'll git jest about fur enough outa camp so's we won't be quite clear o' the stink. This here outfit's goin' to move like every wheel was bogged down in merlasses."

His pessimism was quickly verified. The ponderous business of getting the army into motion began at dawn the following day, the scouts and two companies of the Fifth marching out in reasonably good style. Then came a train of ammunition wagons, each vehicle pulling into its place at the command of a mounted officer who was flanked by two sergeants carrying manifests. A commissary detail followed, each wagon being checked with care as it took its place in the long line which was now winding far to the west along the Missouri's west bank. When a part of Phelps' Light Artillery Battery wheeled into line, it was nearly noon. Half of the day had passed and only a tiny fraction of the entire force had even stirred.

Spencer watched it all lazily from the seat of a wagon. His division was scheduled to move at noon of the following day, but already it was apparent that the orders had been overly optimistic. At the rate those other outfits were getting into line, the Callahan wagons would be a good three days more in camp.

Still Spencer could watch with something more than the disappointment which seemed to be the common reaction. He knew that the commanders had blundered badly, but there was something about the picture which moved him. A sort of nostalgia, perhaps. It was good to see the frenzied activity of dispatch riders and to hear the shouts of troop commanders and wagon bosses. There was an excitement in the plunging of animals against harness, even in the pall of yellow dust which soon shrouded the river front. It brought back memories which were somehow not so bitter as they might have been. A vast organization was moving to accomplish something. Men were working together for a common cause, not heeding the difficulties under which they labored.

Ridiculous thoughts, he scoffed at himself. What good could be said for this scene of confusion? Men were trying to bring order out of chaos by sheer weight of profanity, staff officers cursing unoffending messengers, messengers swearing in turn at teamsters, teamsters venting their accumulated venom on draft animals. It was army nonsense all over again.

Now and then a bugle clamored as some irate commander found it impossible to make his voice heard above the din. Infantrymen moved slowly into position along the line of march, carrying packs and muskets which might just as well have been loaded into the wagons they were assigned to guard. Other infantrymen stood by and grinned at their moving companions, waiting silently in the traditional manner of the soldier who is momentarily unemployed and who doesn't propose to call attention to his happy status.

Horse teams plunged wildly as they rolled their loads into the beaten ruts of the Overland Trail. Ox teams accomplished the same end by slow plodding. Mules balked and kicked but fell into line with the others. The yellow dust settled over everything, invading collars and waistbands until there was no comfort in movement or repose.

Cal Trent was as good as his word. He turned up at the Callahan wagons in the early evening, full of gossip and plainly disgusted with the way matters were going. "We're about five miles west," he told Spencer. "I'm guessin' it'll take four-five days to git the whole column strung out along the trail. We'll reach Salt Lake in mebbe two years."

"It won't be so bad after we get started," Spencer said.

"Don't fool yerself. They've got everything muddled up so that nobody knows nothin'. At the last minute we git word the dragoons ain't even comin' with us. Keepin' 'em to stand guard over the Kansas elections. Ole General Harney's stayin' with 'em. A helluva commander he turned out to be!"

"You sound like the folks in town," Spencer replied, his chuckle almost mirthless. "They seem to think he's playing too much politics to know what he's doing with the army."

"They're plenty right on that! A commander with any sense woulda been movin' the first outfits west all this last month. Now we're all startin' in a lump and tangle."

"It'll straighten out."

"Shore! It'll straighten out into a long line that we ain't got men enough to guard. Won't the Cheyennes and Sioux have theirselves a picnic with that kind of a target!" He spat vigorously and went on. "All the sojers we got is that fool cannon outfit and the Fifth Infantry. The dragoons ain't with us and the Tenth Infantry ain't showed up. We won't have no rear guard at all. Too dam' many wagons fer the number o' men we got."

After another day of watching wagons rolling into line, Spencer decided that Trent was not being unduly fearful. This expedition was spreading itself over a tremendous length of trail. On the night of the nineteenth he rode westward along the line of camps. Since there was no break between the last unit to move and the first one scheduled to take position at dawn, it had the effect of stringing out the original camp for some fifteen miles to the west. That kind of line would be mighty hard to guard in the mountain country.

Shortly after dawn on the twentieth, Spencer saw Donnel's division take its place in line. He noted the position with care, calculating that there would be a good two miles normally between Donnel and him on the line of march. An hour later he was interested to note the departure of a somewhat smaller wagon unit which moved out with a notable lack of noise, the drivers urging on their mules with shouts that were obviously restrained. The ordinary muleskinner language seemed to be a lost art with this outfit, and even the officers who were issuing orders along the line of march lowered their voices a trifle as they sent the division into its proper place.

"Wimmen," McCready grimaced at Spencer's shoulder. "One o' the sojers from the Fifth was tellin' me about seein' the outfit gittin' put together. Officers' wives. Some sergeants' wives what're supposed to be laundry wimmen fer the army. Some gals as ain't proper wives to nobody. And I ain't jest meanin' the one we know about."

"That's army for you," Spencer retorted. "They searched the train to root out all the women who were hiding with the wagoners — but then they send a special division of wagons for them. How are they billed, or didn't you hear?"

McCready laughed aloud, the fat around his middle bouncing with the hilarity. "That part I like," he declared. "I had a peek at the list. They're on the manifests as officers' baggage, washtubs, and assorted camp equipment. I reckon there musta been a joker at headquarters."

Spencer laughed, but he wished that there had been someone with more serious thoughts in charge of this march. July was two-thirds gone and the rear guard of wagons had not yet left Leavenworth.

His outfit moved late on the afternoon of the twentieth, but he knew that not much of an interval separated him from the women's unit. All through the middle of the day movement had been maddeningly slow as stoppages along the line halted everything behind them. Spencer's division moved less than a mile before darkness ended all operations. It meant that the expedition was now strung out nearly twenty miles to the west of Fort Leavenworth, where the Callahan wagons now rested. Behind them another mile of wagons were in line already, while the remaining outfits would certainly make up an additional mile of train. If the dragoons and the missing infantry ever caught up, the line of march would probably be a full twenty-five miles in length.

It reminded Spencer of what Trent had said about the army being a fine target for Indian raids. In the back of his mind he knew another kind of apprehension. In case the Mormons decided to resist the invasion, their mounted militia would have it easy.

The next few days were just as dusty, just as tedious, just as wearying. The train inched forward slowly, gaps beginning to open up as slow units blocked those following. Spencer remained with his wagons, watching progress and estimating the way his men were shaping up. This was routine here on the prairie; he wanted to know what kind of crew he had before they reached the Platte crossing. That would be the test of the bullwhacker. The teamsters who showed their mettle at that point would be dependable in the rugged passes of the mountains.

It heartened him a little to find every man in the crew doing his work quite well. He and McCready spelled off the drivers in turn so that each man in the crew could get a little relief each day. It wasn't necessary here in Kansas but it was a routine which Spencer wished to have established. Later it would be helpful and he wanted the men to feel that the whole crew was organized to be mutually helpful.

At the Platte crossing, he found time to ride ahead and inspect the tangle which had developed there. Wagons were bunching up on the near side of the treacherous stream, forming a jam which had already halted traffic a good two miles to the rear. He saw Curt

Donnel at a distance but was content to avoid the man for the present. Sooner or later the crooked trader would make his play; that would be soon enough for action.

He had known a vague hope that he might speak with the English girl, but he did not press the matter when he saw that the wagon division in question was being kept to one side, well guarded by soldiers of the Fifth. Evidently the officers who had arranged the plan were not taking any chances on a surprise inspection east of the mountains.

Spencer returned to his wagons disgruntled but in a general way satisfied. For the moment at least he did not have to divide his attention from his real duty. As to the future — he could only recall with uneasiness that the season was getting steadily later. The army should have been across the Platte by the end of May, not the end of July.

CHAPTER NINE

During the week following the platte crossing, progress was good. Twice Spencer rode ahead in the evening to look at the two units in which he was most interested, but on neither occasion did the trip prove worth while. The second ride even turned out to be dangerous because sentries challenged him all along the line. An Indian alarm was reported and the guard detail was inclined to be suspicious. On the following morning an order was passed along the line that all men would remain with their own units in order that sentries might not mistake them for marauders. It ended Spencer's chance of doing any personal scouting but it also had the effect of checking any schemes Curt Donnel might have entertained.

That evening the Callahan men were gathered around their cooking fires after the usual supper of sowbelly and biscuit. Most of them were showing signs of weariness, but there had been little sickness in the outfit, a bit of good fortune largely attributable to the absent Callahan. As an Irishman who liked his tea, he always encouraged his men to drink the beverage. Thus they did not use the wretched water of the region and avoided the dysentery which seemed to be striking at every other unit in the army.

Talk turned partly to the Indian rumors but mostly the men talked about the fast pace which they had been making of late. The officers in command were now getting miracles done, evidently realizing that much ground had to be made up to offset the slow start. Even through the sandy wastes along the lower Platte the train had averaged an unbelievable thirty miles per day. It was excellent progress, but the draft animals were showing the effects and the men were sobered by the realization that they might lose valuable stock.

Shortly after supper Cal Trent dropped in. He had been assigned to patrol this section of the line, he announced as he took a seat beside the fire and proceeded to light an ancient pipe. This did not seem like the sort of activity which might be expected of a man on scout duty, but Spencer knew Trent well enough not to ask questions. If Cal had decided to sit out his patrol, he probably had a good enough reason.

O'Rourke was not so well informed on the Trent character. He looked up from a piece of harness he was mending, his grunt openly critical. "Did ye expect to find Injuns here — or would ye be waitin' fer the heathen to come git us?"

Trent did not look around. He took a couple of solemn puffs at his pipe before remarking, "Some folks ain't got no more gumption than officers. Ain't a red injun this side o' Chimney Rock, I'll lay to that. Wild talk and skittishness, that's what it is."

"Who ordered the extra guards?" Spencer inquired.

Trent shrugged. "Who knows? They ain't nobuddy in charge o' this dam' army nohow. Harney ain't never ketched up to us. None o' the understrappers know who's supposed to take charge. They're all shovin' a hot pertater around because they're plumb worried. Mostly because them extry troops ain't comin' up behind us yit."

"You mean the dragoons?"

"Partly. The Tenth Infantry fellers ain't come up yet nuther."

"Then we don't have a rear guard?"

"All we need, I reckon. We got a dozen fellers back there with some o' the new Springfields that they ain't issued to troops yit. They'll be plenty — since there ain't no redskins prowlin' around nohow."

Trent remained in the Callahan camp all night, but Spencer was a little disappointed when he could get no news of consequence out of the old trapper. Cal talked volubly about the new rifled musket which had been issued to a few good marksmen among the infantry units and to the detachment of scouts who were serving as rear guard. He seemed to feel that its five hundred grain hollow slug would be of much greater value than the artillery. On every other subject he had no comment. With Cal Trent that was final.

The weather continued favorable and as the August days ran behind them so did Chimney Rock, Scott's Bluff, and the adobe walls of Old Fort Laramie. Progress had been better than Spencer had anticipated, but then the character of the country changed and they began to work into the tortuous trails of the Black Hills country, home of the hostile Sioux. Cal Trent did not appear as a visitor very often now; he was on the alert with the other scouts, spying out the country on all sides of the long, vulnerable train of wagons.

No one needed to be reminded that danger lurked around them. The trail was well marked by pathetic relics of earlier trains. At this point the emigrants' optimism had begun to ebb and they had started to face stark necessity by lightening their loads. Cherished belongings, already freighted halfway across a continent, had been discarded here as men fought to keep weary animals going. Ornately carved furniture, rusty plows, four-poster beds, broken trunks and other items of family pride littered the trail side. Here the early emigrants had begun to appreciate the real difficulty of the task ahead. "Heartbreak stretch," some of them had called it. Here some had bitterly regretted the decision to come west. Here some had ceased to have regrets — their crudely fashioned grave markers were all too frequent.

Independence Rock fell behind. Now they were out of Sioux Country, working along the Sweetwater, where the only Indians were the friendly Crows. Still each camp had to be carefully guarded, the thieving friendlies causing more trouble than aloof hostiles. It was at one of the night camps in the Crow country that Spencer received his first reminder that he still had a personal problem on his hands.

He was taking his turn as night guard, shortly before midnight, somewhat to the right of the line of march. Suddenly a rifle cracked in the darkness and a slug tore at the sleeve of Spencer's shirt. He went down at once, lying flat on the grass as he tried to locate his assailant.

The camp was in instant uproar, but the fact was of no help at all. The noise merely kept Spencer from locating a sound which might indicate a retreating attacker and he muttered disgustedly as men gathered around him. They made a brief search in the darkness but it was a waste of time. He would have to regard the attack as a warning and take more precautions in future.

Three days later Cal Trent rode beside him for a short distance, passing on a bit of gossip. "Got a new quartermaster," he announced. "Old fool name of Burns. I reckon he's a mite teched in the head."

"What happened to Van Vliet?"

"He pushed on ahead to make some arrangements at Salt Lake. Must be he's fixin' it so's Brigham Young and the Mormon elders will be rollin' out a red carpet fer us."

"How do you mean that? Is everything peaceful or are you being sarcastic?"

The older man grinned. "I ain't rightly knowin', Spence. We don't hear of no signs o' trouble, but I can't figger them Mormons is goin' to let us in without a fuss."

"You're a calamity howler, Cal."

"I reckon so. But I ain't celebratin' none yet." Then he added almost grudgingly. "Them two companies of the Tenth is back there with the rear guard now. That oughta make some folks feel a mite safer."

"Any word of General Harney and the dragoons?"

"Nope. Still watchin' Kansas elections, I reckon."

The third week of September saw them through the back-breaking haul of the South Pass. Animals died daily and were butchered for fresh meat. Even stringy old oxen offered a change from so much salt pork. The supply of spare animals was dwindling to the critical point, but the worst of the haul was over. The bulk of the train was rolling down-grade into the valley of Green River. Dry Sandy, Little Sandy, Big Sandy — all became minor obstacles in the light of what had already been passed. The Utah line was not many days ahead now. Perhaps the expedition would fool everyone and reach its objective before snow could impede progress.

Evidently this was the important point in the minds of the several commanders who, lacking a real command, now had assumed charge of various units. They began to move their outfits forward more rapidly, leaving the wagons almost unguarded. The belated companies of the Tenth even deserted their posts as rear guard and hurried forward to join the regiments pressing forward into Utah. It was not a situation for the happiness of wagon drivers, but no one considered them.

On the twenty-eighth of September, one day following the forward movement of the Tenth Infantry units, a brisk young lieutenant wheeled his horse in beside Spencer as he flanked his wagon division. "You the leader of this outfit?" he inquired abruptly.

"I am. Why?"

"Your name Corliss?"

"No."

The lieutenant seemed surprised and a little annoyed. “That’s odd,” he said. “I thought sure . . .” He broke off and glanced at some papers he had drawn from a pocket. “Callahan wagons. Daniel Spencer in charge. Are you Spencer?”

“Now you got it. What’s all this about?”

A quizzical light came into the young fellow’s eyes as he looked sideways at Spencer. “I guess I won’t ask too many questions. Names don’t mean much on this party, I imagine. All I want to tell you is that somebody better take care of a Mrs. Corliss up at the washtub division.”

“What’s wrong with her?” Spencer asked quickly, not bothering to work out the odd series of mistakes which seemed to be back of the officer’s remarks.

“Nothing wrong with her. It’s just that old Burns, the new quartermaster, has been throwing his authority around. He must have been the only officer in the army who didn’t know about our consignment of officers’ baggage and washtubs. Yesterday he happened to stumble on it because some of the officers in Phelps’ battery were trying to get their wives into their own wagons so they could pull out ahead of the train. Now the fat’s in the fire and Major Burns is threatening to send every woman back to Kansas. We’re passing the word to the men concerned so they can get their gals into safer quarters.”

Spencer studied his man carefully, making certain that the young officer was not trying to be funny. Then he said, “You’ve got things mixed up somewhere. There’s no one named Corliss with this outfit. We’ve got a pair of wagons with us that belong to a Miss Corliss but —"

"You don't need to be too careful with me," the lieutenant interrupted. "It just happens that I was with Cap'n Marcy when Mr. Callahan made his deal. He wanted to hire a fellow named Corliss to boss this string of wagons. Corliss wouldn't take on the chore because he had a couple of wagons of his own and he wanted to bring his wife along. Cap'n Marcy agreed to let the woman ride with the other ladies, the Corliss wagons to join this division. That was the deal and I remember it well, so don't try to push me off. Just pass the word to this fellow Corliss. Tell him to get his wife clear or she'll be ridin' an empty grub wagon back to Kansas."

In spite of the firmness of his tone, the lieutenant seemed to think it was all quite humorous. He waved briskly at Spencer with the final statement then galloped away before any reply could be made. Spencer didn't have much to say that would have been informative — unless someone happened to be interested in a colorful description of the character, antecedents, and general deceitfulness of Anvil Callahan.

He was still talking to himself when he urged his mount forward, but the conversation was not quite so violent now. He could understand the difficulty Callahan might have had in making a place for the English girl in the baggage train. Probably the Irishman had been forced to trifle a bit with the truth in order to obtain army consent — but it was nothing but Callahan cussedness that had made him hit upon this particular yarn!

There was nothing to be done about it now, however. Callahan was out of reach — probably chuckling maliciously at the thought of the trick he had pulled. But Miss Corliss was in danger of being shipped east just when she was within striking distance of her objective. Spencer knew that he would not see her thwarted if he could avoid it. Matters might grow a bit awkward if he had to conceal her in his wagon division, but he knew that he would have to give it a try.

He found a show of activity around the wagon unit in question, but when he asked for Miss Corliss he was met by a firm shake of the head. "Got nobuddy left by that name," an infantry sergeant told him. "Ain't got many at all. They're gittin' out fast before anything kin happen. I got my old lady away in a hurry — but I was right on hand to know what was goin' on."

"Do you know where Miss Corliss went?"

"I can't be exack sure. Too much hustle and bustle around here in the last few hours. I reckon she rode for'ard with another lady. Some cap'n's wife, I kinda think it was."

"Fine," Spencer told him. "That's all I wanted to know."

He felt a little let down as he slowly rode back to his own outfit. He knew that it had worked out to his own best interests. Having a woman along at this stage of the march could turn out to be troublesome. That was what he told himself — but he didn't believe what he heard. In spite of his own judgment, he had been looking forward to seeing the girl again. It was a fact which he knew he ought to face even though it disturbed him a little.

No further word came to him although rumors were running along the line in abundance. They didn't concern women now; men were talking about an increasingly persistent report that the army was to rendezvous at the crossing of the Green River, there to await some word from Major Van Vliet or a direct order from the lagging commander, General Harney. The various regimental officers did not care to push on into Utah Territory without some specific instructions.

Spencer's unit reached the Green crossing late on the afternoon of the fifth of October. Other wagons were making the crossing but none were halting. Nor were there any troops in sight except the sprinkling of guards who were always posted at such crossings. A staff lieutenant who intimated that his information had come from Colonel Alexander of the Tenth Infantry informed each teamster that all wagons were to concentrate on Ham's Fork, some thirty miles beyond the Green. There the army would halt for reorganization.

Dusk fell before Spencer could get any of his wagons into the ford, so he held back to let several vehicles of a smaller outfit go through. It permitted him to keep his entire unit on the near side of the Green, a precaution he chose to take rather than to split it. Sight of the infantrymen withdrawing up the trail at sundown made him a little sorry for his decision, but there seemed to be no cause for alarm. No savages had demonstrated even at a distance for several days.

Spencer took one of the early watches, trying to give wagoners at least a short rest before any of them went on duty. He found the night as silent as preceding ones had been. A hint of crispness in the air warned that the summer was certainly over. He stood his watch for three hours, then roused McCready and rolled in his blanket, the comforting warmth putting him to sleep at once.

When he awoke he had a feeling that he had closed his eyes for only an instant, but that something had gone wrong in that instant. Somewhere close at hand a man cursed sharply and bitterly, warning him that the feeling was not a mere figment of dreams. Spencer rolled clear of his blanket with a gun in his hand.

Even as he moved a voice snapped, "Don't git rash, brother. We got ye covered and we'll shoot if'n we have to."

By that time he was able to see the scene around him. Four of his teamsters were seated on the ground by a dying fire while others were being herded out from their sleeping places by bearded men with guns. Spencer could count at least a dozen of the intruders in sight and he could hear the muttered commands of others as they worked among the wagons. Without a word he shoved his six-shooter into his belt, hoping that no one had noticed.

A voice behind him chuckled dryly. "Jest so ye keep it there, brother. We ain't amin' to hurt nobody so don't start a fight ye can't hope to win. Hustle it up, over there, make sure we got every man outa them wagons!"

"What is all this?" Spencer inquired, trying to keep his voice calm.

"This is a raid, sir," a bearded, middle-aged man informed him gravely. "We are militia of the Latter Day Saints. We strike with fire but not with sword — unless obliged to do so. You will please avoid any resistance."

"What the hell kind of a raid do yuh call that?" one of the bullwhackers demanded. "Of all the dam' — !"

"No blasphemy, sir!" the bearded man barked. "Hurry up there, men. Fire the wagons as soon as you make certain no living soul remains in them."

"You're making a mistake," Spencer told him conversationally. "These wagons are under contract to the United States army. They'll be real put-out if they have a damage claim to setttle."

"I fully understand," the Morman leader said with quiet dignity. "The United States has made a mistake in bringing force into the territory. We deplore force. My orders are to destroy these symbols of tyranny."

Spencer didn't insist. He decided that a man who could talk like that under the present circumstances was not likely to be in the mood for any sort of argument. Just now the Mormon had all the arguments on his side — about twenty of them, all armed.

CHAPTER TEN

The raiders worked fast but without undue haste. Several stern-looking men held Spencer and his drivers at gun point while the others went through the camp collecting weapons and personal property from each wagon. Then they carried brands from the fire around the circle and soon each wagon was in flames. Sight of the leaping fires caused the wagon drivers to mutter angrily, but Spencer restrained them. "No time to argue," he cautioned. "They hold all the cards."

"A piece of wisdom," the Mormon leader commented. "Even though uttered in the language of the devil." For a moment Spencer didn't get the point but then he realized the man was referring to the mention of cards. It seemed a bit odd that a man who considered cards as instruments of the devil should feel so free about burning up public property.

Still under guard, the prisoners were led clear of the burning wagons and then Spencer could see another glare in the sky to the east. The raid had not been concentrated on this one wagon division alone; the Mormons had struck at other spots as well. He wondered what had dictated the choice of targets.

The bearded leader snapped a couple of crisp commands, halting the prisoners where the firelight was still strong. Then he whistled a shrill, wavering note. Almost at once the clatter of hoofs sounded above the crackle of burning wagons.

"We will leave you now," the Mormon said quietly. "At the shore of the river we will leave your personal belongings and your weapons. A man with a rifle will watch from the other shore to see that you do not try to reach them until my men have had ten minutes' start. Do you understand?"

"Reasonable enough," Spencer agreed, determined to be philosophic over a matter he could not argue. "Decent of you to leave us our own duffle."

"We do not war on our fellow men," the Mormon stated. "Only on the government which tries to enslave us."

Before anyone could offer a comment, the rider who had been whistled in from outpost duty appeared in the increasing light from the holocaust. It was Spencer's turn to whistle. "McGee! I thought you were heading for the west coast."

The lanky trapper looked uneasily about him. "I kinda intended that," he admitted. "Seemed as how folks sorta shoved me into this. Nobody seemed to like Mormons 'cept Mormons. I reckon ye kin see how it was."

"Sure. But you're itching for real trouble now."

McGee grinned. "We ain't doin' so bad, I reckon. Got a smart feller name of Lot Smith runnin' our army. Who ye got to match him with your'n?"

Spencer ignored the thrust. It was evident that the Mormons were quite aware that the invading army was hampered by lack of a commander. "So you're determined on war, are you?" he asked.

The bearded man took the talk away from McGee. "War is an abomination," he intoned. "We war on no one. But we will destroy the goods of those who propose to bring iniquity to Deseret. You may pass that word. To your horses, men; our task is done here!"

No word was spoken as the raiders slipped away into the outer circles of light, finally to disappear across the ford of the Green. Then it was Ned O'Rouke who said wonderingly, "Ain't that the craziest bunch o' galoots ye've ever seen? Or ain't they so dam' crazy at that?"

"Indians are kinda crazy, one way you think about it," Spencer commented. "But it doesn't make them a bit less dangerous. Sit tight now and give them the time they asked for. At this point we don't need to be in any big hurry." He looked around the circle of men soberly as he asked, "Who was on picket duty when they showed up?"

Tom Jonas sheepishly admitted that he was the unwary guard who had been surprised. "Jest like Injuns they was," he grumbled. "I never hear a danged thing 'til a feller pokes a gun in my ribs and tells me to h'ist my paws. They seemed real sociable when I didn't kick up no fuss. Not that it woulda done much good. The rest of 'em was in camp almost as soon as I got ketched."

"What did they do with the stock?"

"Jest run 'em off. Seemed like they was plumb careful not to steal anything."

Several other voices broke in to relate incidents they had noticed and Spencer let the talk go for a couple of minutes, giving the men a chance to blow off some of their pent-up steam. He was about to halt them with orders to move when his ear caught a distant sound which came clear above the roar of flames and the crackle of excited conversation. A rider was angling toward the ford from a spot almost directly north of the burning camp.

He held up a hand for silence. "Listen. Didn't that Mormon say they would leave their picket on the other side of the Green?"

No one replied. They were listening to the hoofbeats. A rider had dashed for the ford and had gone on across, moving much too hastily for good judgment. Even allowing for the illumination provided by the raiders, he was risking a lot to cross the Green in darkness at such speed.

"Too late," Spencer said as one of the men started to run toward the river. "But I wonder who he was and what he was doing out there. Mac, you'd better take the boys and try to round up the stock. I'll go on down to the ford and see what our visitors left us. After that somebody will have to fork a nag and ride up ahead to pass the word."

A rider pounded up the trail from the rear while they were carrying out his orders and he heard the details of another raid similar to the one he had just witnessed. The Mormons there had been less voluble but they had operated in the same manner. No shot had been fired. The whole thing had been a complete surprise and a success for the raiders. Between the two places some thirty wagons had been burned.

"No troops here," Spencer told him. "Wait a bit 'til my men round up a horse for me and I'll go ahead with you. Maybe this fire has been seen by some of the sentinels at the military camps — and maybe it hasn't."

"If yuh'll do the tellin', I'll git back," the messenger retorted. "I got things to do — and I ain't too keen on answerin' a lot o' fool questions."

He wheeled and rode back along the trail without giving Spencer a chance to argue. Not that it mattered very much. One report would do the trick — such as it was. A glare in the sky to the southwest hinted that even one report from the Green crossing might not be needed. Somebody closer to Ham's Fork had been a victim.

Still Spencer took the first horse brought in; he used a blanket to replace the saddle which had gone up in smoke with the rest of the equipment. He crossed the ford without mishap, and rode carefully along the dark trail until a bend took him into complete blackness. Then he had to grope his way along, wondering whether the Mormon militia had come this way or whether they had cut off on some trail known only to themselves.

After a mile of slow progress he sighted a camp ahead, undoubtedly the outfit which had been last to cross the Green on the previous afternoon. Men were awake around a couple of fires and he paused only long enough to answer a few questions. They had seen fire ahead, but had seen no sign of the Mormons and did not know of the troubles beyond the Green, for the mountains cut off their view of the spot.

After that Spencer rode past one outfit after another until he rounded an outcropping to stare at another circle of glowing embers. Here a wagon outfit had made its protective circle for the night. Here it had been put to the torch. Again he halted only long enough to trade stories, learning that a messenger had gone to report. The Tenth Infantry's headquarters was supposed to be only a few miles ahead.

Spencer moved on, his mind beginning to grapple with some of the problems which he had not at first considered. What would he do now that there was no longer a wagon train to handle? Could his men get back out of the mountains before snowfall? Where was Curt Donnel? Where was Miss Corliss?

It was helpless thinking. He knew that none of the answers would be forthcoming immediately, but he could not keep himself from asking them. He had been hoping for developments that would offer him some solution to his own problem; instead he was now having to consider the problems of an army suddenly harassed by an efficient and energetic enemy.

Just before dawn he was challenged by a sleepy sentry and twenty minutes later he was telling his story to Captain Marcy. He had asked for that officer even though he did not expect to find him there, figuring that the officers of the Tenth would pay a little more heed to a man who seemed to know someone. It turned out that the camp on Ham's Fork was occupied chiefly by the Fifth, and only two companies of the Tenth were there.

Marcy listened with frowning interest but not without asking a few personal questions about Spencer's activities as wagon boss. Then he said abruptly, "We've had a report of a raid from another outfit. That would be the one you passed. Nobody paid much attention; the rider was drunk."

Spencer did not reply. It seemed to him that the military commander was pretty lax to let that sort of report go unheeded, regardless of the condition of the messenger, but he knew better than to say so.

"We'll go see Colonel Alexander," Marcy told him then. "Don't be surprised if he's a mite testy. Just now he's ready to skin almost anybody. He doesn't have a scrap of authority over anyone but his own Tenth Infantry, but he's senior officer and all the decisions fall upon him. He knows that he'll be damned for everything he does and everything he doesn't do."

"He has my sympathy," Spencer said dryly.

"Forget that," Marcy advised. "Believe me, I'm not too pleased with the way things have gone. Just as I thought I'd been doing a good job as a scout officer they sent me back to my old command and put a greenhorn in as scout commander."

"I heard," Spencer told him. "Cal Trent told me — between cusses."

It took a little time to get to Colonel Alexander, but when that officer was fully awake he took quick action, only complaining a little at the necessity.

Captain Marcy was to take four hundred men, mostly from the Fifth, and return to bring up the remnants of the wagon train. Each man was to carry field rations and fifty rounds of ammunition, but only a small detachment from each company was to be mounted. They were to take no offensive action, but all wagons were to be brought forward under guard to the rendezvous on Ham's Fork.

Same old story, Spencer thought as he watched the preparations going forward. These precautions should have been observed from the beginning — and more men should be mounted. For years the army had failed to realize the futility of sending infantry against mounted Indians and they were repeating the error in preparing to defend against the Mormon militia. Even now the few infantrymen who had been converted into cavalry were on surplus mules. Against those well-mounted and well-disciplined mountaineers from Salt Lake, they would be as futile as infantry.

"Our outfit's got surplus oxen now that the wagons are gone," Spencer murmured in an aside to Marcy. "Do you suppose somebody will think it a smart idea to put foot-sloggers on some of the bulls? That'd give the Mormons a good laugh."

Marcy shook his head disgustedly. "Will you ride along with me, Spencer?" he asked. "I'm taking a few of the best mounted men and heading back at once. I'd appreciate your advice."

Spencer nodded, again recognizing the feeling of mutual respect which had earlier appeared in his relations with the infantry officer. "I'll be glad to.

Maybe you can give me some help on a problem of mine later. There's a lady named Corliss in camp somewhere and I imagine she's going to need a bit of help. I'd like to find her — after this mess is untangled."

Marcy regarded him with surprised interest. Then he smiled. "I don't blame you," he said. "And I know where she is." He didn't say any more about her but his show of good humor hinted that he was pleased to find that Spencer had an interest in the camp. Only when they were riding along the back trail did he come out and say so. "Glad you'll be coming back with me, Spencer," he said frankly. "We'll need you. The scout outfit is up ahead somewhere — trying to guess what sort of trouble the Mormons are preparing."

"Then you knew that they were getting ready to strike?"

"Not until last evening. We thought it was going to be easy."

"Have you heard anything from Major Van Vliet?" Spencer asked, trying to fit the two statements together.

"That's what fooled us. Van Vliet came back to us day before yesterday. He reported that there would be no opposition to our march into the territory. Last night, however, a rider came in to give us an entirely different picture. Two days after the major left Salt Lake, Brigham Young issued a proclamation in which he denounced this army as brigands and forbade it to enter the territory. At the same time he called upon all Mormons to take up arms in defense of their community."

"That's a fast switch," Spencer commented. "Almost a three-way tie between a peace report, a declaration of war, and some well-organized raids. Too bad we can't find some kind of commander who'll be half as efficient."

Marcy did not seem disposed to reply. He might be pretty bitter about General Harney's decision to remain in Kansas and play politics, but as an officer under orders he did not propose to commit himself.

They met a courier just before they reached Green River. The man brought word that the Mormon cavalry had destroyed a third wagon train on the Big Sandy. Their surprise raid had been just as swift as the ones on the Green. No shots had been fired and no one had been hurt.

Actually the report amounted to a bit of extra information, the courier having originally been sent forward by Colonel Smith of the Tenth. Smith and the missing companies of the Tenth were on the Sweetwater and the message was a relay from Kansas to the effect that the Second Dragoons were finally moving west to join the expedition.

Marcy accepted the news stoically although Spencer suspected that he wanted to curse. Here was an additional reminder of Harney's stupid carelessness. Had those dragoons been riding patrols along the line — as should have been the case — the Mormons would not have had such an easy time of it.

"What's your advice, Spencer?" Captain Marcy asked. "You know the situation at least as well as I do

— and you know the country better. What is our next move?"

"Just what we're doing now," Spencer told him. "I suppose this man will have to take his message on to Colonel Alexander. We'll grab the first mounted men we can find and send them back along the line to tell every wagon outfit to fort up and stay that way until Smith's companies reach them. Then the wagons can move up under convoy."

"You heard that," Marcy said quietly, turning to the waiting soldier. "Tell Colonel Alexander that it is necessary. Ask him to make it an official order to Brevet-Colonel Smith. And ask him to issue the order quickly."

When the courier was on his way again Marcy grimaced briefly at Spencer. "Army red-tape," he grumbled. "Smith out-ranks me but Alexander out-ranks him. This way we'll be sure he doesn't come on through without keeping every wagon under guard."

This time it was Spencer's turn to make no comment. None was needed.

They spent a busy day at the crossing of the Green, Marcy making it his headquarters while he detailed his units to various guard duties and sent other riders back along the trail with warnings. By nightfall fifty wagons had crossed the stream and were moving on toward Ham's Fork under infantry guard. Still other trains were camped short of the river, all of them bunched for protection with soldiers acting as pickets. The Mormon raiders would not have an easy time of it if they elected to try new raids this night.

Meanwhile Spencer had not been idle. He managed to locate three partly empty provision wagons and loaded everything they carried into one. Then he sent his own crew back over the trail with the two empties, warning them first that they must make good time on the back trail if they hoped to get out of the mountains before the first snows. It was a move he did not like to make. It committed him to remaining with the army, but he knew that he would not have it otherwise. There were at least two good reasons why he had to stay.

At dusk he rode along the line with Captain Marcy, checking the positions of the guards and making certain that every wagon unit was closed up in the best defense position available. Several times during the afternoon Mormon militiamen had been seen on the distant slopes. Perhaps they were simply scouts watching the invading army, but just as likely they were spies searching for new targets. The Mormon declaration of war had been no idle gesture and men all along the line were preparing for defense.

"They've already hit us hard," Marcy said thoughtfully. "I've had complete reports now on their first raids and they seem to have made only one mistake."

"What was that?"

"Maybe it was just chance but they seemed to pick trains that were hauling food. Your outfit had flour, along with those spare uniforms and extra harness. Classen's wagons carried bacon. The wagons back there on the Big Sandy had quite a variety of stuff in them. We've lost our entire stock of tools and implements for building, most of our horse medicines, some stationery and cooking utensils, and a couple of additional loads of clothing."

"Sounds like smart raiding to me. What was their mistake?"

"They just missed the main body of clothing wagons. If they'd struck a little farther east they'd have had us in a bad state."

"We're not too well off as it is," Spencer reminded him. "Several hundred pairs of boots went up in smoke right here last night."

The following morning a small train passed to the east. It was made up of wagons which had been emptied of supplies and which now were carrying men unfit for service. Quartermaster Van Vliet rode with them, on his way east to deliver the conflicting messages he carried. At the same time he brought word for Captain Marcy to return to Ham's Fork for orders.

That suited Spencer well enough. If other wagons were working east, his own men would not be in any danger of being isolated for any length of time by either mishap or early snow. He could forget about them and put all his attention on the things he needed to think about here.

It was well that he could find that brief moment of relief. On arrival at Colonel Alexander's headquarters he was not to find matters so easy.

CHAPTER ELEVEN

A cold, menacing darkness had fallen across the mountains by the time they reached the camp on Ham's Fork. No snow was in the air yet but Spencer had a feeling that it would not be long in coming. Before long the army would have something more than Mormon raiders to worry about.

He had suggested attaching himself to one of the wagon outfits, but Captain Marcy had vetoed the suggestion at once, insisting that Spencer should accompany him to Colonel Alexander's tent. "You're our only scout just now," he said. "Lieutenant Bickford is somewhere up ahead so we'll need a man who knows the mountains. I'm depending on you."

Spencer did not argue. It had been increasingly clear that he was committing himself with every action to service as a civilian scout. Having sent his own crew back to Kansas he had in effect burned his bridges behind him. Now it made good sense to let Marcy present him to the man who was in temporary command of the expedition. His own freedom of movement would be increased a great deal by clarifying his position in the command.

Marcy broke in on his thoughts, a smile quirking the brown beard as he added, "After we talk to the colonel I want you to come along with me to our adjutant's wagons. Miss Corliss is there."

"You know about her then?"

"Enough to be impolitely curious. Major Pierce, the adjutant, is a pretty good friend of mine and I heard the story just after he had to do a bit of hustling around to get his wife clear. There seems to be something of a mystery in the girl's situation."

"You mean you don't know why she is with the army?"

"No. We understand that part. She has told her story to all of us. The queer part is the rumor that she is married to someone in the baggage train. When the other wives were being hurried away by their husbands she told Mrs. Pierce that there was nowhere for her to go. Mrs. Pierce promptly took charge but without asking any prying questions. The major and I tried to look up a possible husband but could find nothing more than a definite impression that such a man existed — and in your wagon train. I was forced to the conclusion today — after seeing the rest of your men sent east — that you must be the mysterious spouse."

Spencer chuckled dryly, aware that Marcy was hinting for information. "Do you know Anvil Callahan?" he inquired.

"I know of him. Why?"

"Because if you know him the explanation is easy. Anvil fancies himself as a conniver and this seems to have been one of his more ambitious efforts." He told the story as he knew it, realizing that Marcy was reading something more into it. Obviously the officer believed that Spencer was playing down his own part in the arrangements.

Marcy announced himself and Spencer when they reached Colonel Alexander's tent and a murmur of conversation broke off at once. Then a sharp voice sounded. "Bring Spencer in here, Captain!" It sounded ominously like an order.

Two men were in the big tent, both of them keeping close to a camp stove. Colonel Alexander was seated on a chest with a camp table in front of him while at one side of the table appeared a lean, angry-eyed officer of perhaps thirty-five. His brown beard was neatly trimmed and his uniform was just a trifle too immaculate for a man on field duty. The insignia identified him as a captain in the Quartermaster Corps.

"Major Burns has just brought me some disturbing intelligence," Colonel Alexander stated grimly. "Now that you are here I'd like him to repeat it."

The confusion of titles did not bother Spencer too much. He was well aware that many officers who had been promoted during the Mexican War had been forced to serve in lower ranks in the peacetime army. Brevet-Colonel Smith, for example, was probably acting as a Major in the Tenth. Captain Burns was being given his social rank rather than his official one now. What was surprising was that the man should appear so young. Cal Trent had referred to him as an old fool.

"Captain Marcy," the lean man said harshly, "I have just been given to understand that this man you are using as your aide is of questionable character." He scarcely glanced at Spencer as he spoke.

Marcy kept his voice calm. "If you are referring to Spencer's war record, I probably know more about it than either you or your informant."

"War record?" Burns echoed, obviously puzzled. "Now you are talking riddles, sir."

"Then let's solve your riddle first," Marcy agreed quietly, covering his mistake in a hurry. "What is so questionable about him?"

"A short time ago I was handed a message. It was not well written, was not signed, and seems to have come through several pairs of hands before reaching me. Ordinarily I might ignore it but under present circumstances we cannot afford to be careless.

"The message states," Captain Burns went on, "that the Mormons who burned Spencer's wagon train were clearly friends of his. They talked in quite familiar fashion while the wagons were being fired. Neither Spencer nor his men made any moves to thwart their efforts. Nor was any pursuit attempted. Finally, it appears that a trapping partner of this man Spencer was in the ranks of the Mormon militia. There seems every reason to suspect that the whole thing was contrived to permit the destruction of that particular wagon division."

Suddenly Spencer remembered that mysterious horseman who had forded the Green on the heels of the Mormons. It had not been a Mormon rear guard at all. Without much doubt one of Donnel's thugs had tried to sneak up on the camp but had been forced to lie low when the raiders struck. His report had been relayed to Burns by Donnel himself. It was guesswork, of course, but Spencer felt certain that he was not far from complete accuracy.

Then he realized that the three officers were staring at him in grim silence. "You want a statement from me, gentlemen?" he inquired, keeping his voice as calm as possible.

Colonel Alexander looked a little surprised at the phrasing of the question but answered with complete civility. "I think it would be in order."

"Very well. Your informant was right. My men and I talked quite a little with the raiders. There was nothing else we could do. They made it clear that they preferred to avoid bloodshed. Since we were on the wrong end of all the guns in sight, we quite agreed with them. They were very decent about it, leaving us our weapons and personal belongings but covering their retreat so that we were helpless until they were clear away. I have already explained this in some detail to Captain Marcy."

Alexander accepted Marcy's prompt nod of substantiation but he asked, "What about the charge that you have a partner among the Mormons?"

"Quite true. Captain Marcy will remember the man. Mormon McGee, Captain, the man who refused to join the scout company at Leavenworth. I might add that I have not seen him since we left Kansas." Shooting a sidelong glance at Captain Burns, he added, "I might also add that we made no arrangements to meet in the future or to work together."

"This all sounds pretty suspicious to me," Burns declared. "Colonel, I should like to suggest that this man be placed under guard."

"Just a minute," Captain Marcy cut in. "I know this man and I tell you it's a mistake to —"

"Several mistakes here," Spencer interrupted. "I don't believe I am subject to army discipline in any event. I'm a contractor's agent. My duty is to my principal only. No official state of war exists — so that the army has no authority over me at all. Please remember that."

"Don't try to be a lawyer out here in the mountains!" Burns snapped.

"Then don't talk like a fool!" Spencer came back at him. "I owned a share in that wagon train. Do you think I'd trade real property for a lawsuit against the government? That's exactly what happened. If you're trying to find someone to blame for the losses of last evening, you'd better look around the Quartermaster Corps. Find the man who loaded everything in wholesale lots instead of distributing various things throughout the entire train. Find the officers who permitted all of the troops to desert the train! Find the commander who never bothered to command! But don't make damn fool charges!"

Captain Burns was on his feet before the tirade was half over. His lean features were contorted behind the trim beard and for a moment Spencer wondered if the man would be foolish enough to try a physical attack.

The spasm passed, however, and Burns kept his tone almost under control as he barked, "Colonel, I request that this man be placed under arrest at once."

Alexander kept his head. It was clear that he was puzzled and a little annoyed, but it was also evident that he realized the ticklish nature of the legalities involved. "I'm not sure that would be in order, Major," he said quietly.

"May I make a suggestion?" Marcy interrupted. "I will take full responsibility for Spencer. Captain Burns may consider him paroled in my custody if the idea will please him."

Alexander almost grinned as he asked, "Does that suit you, Spencer? Or do you want to argue that one?"

"It'll do well enough," Spencer told him easily. "I don't want to embarrass you or Captain Marcy."

"Meaning that you don't care about me?" Burns snapped.

"Not a bit. Should I?" The clear insolence of it almost brought on another outburst, but Colonel Alexander took charge then, bringing the meeting to an end. "Your orders stand, Marcy," he said. "Keep those wagons moving as rapidly as you can with safety. That is all, gentlemen. Captain Burns, I want an inventory of available supplies as soon as you can arrange it."

They were well clear of the tent before Marcy gave Spencer a wink and commented, "You twisted his tail proper, Dan. But you've made an enemy."

"I've got worse ones," Spencer told him quietly, "and not too far away." It was the first time Marcy had ever called him by his first name and he didn't know whether to like the idea or not. It was good to feel that the officer was accepting him as a friend but he wasn't sure that he should encourage it. A man like Marcy had worries enough of his own without involving himself in the troubles of Dan Spencer.

Evidently the infantryman was headed in that very direction for he followed up the comment. "Do you mean that you have enemies in the train? Would one of them be the man you are trying to trap?"

Spencer smiled in the darkness. Marcy hadn't forgotten anything — and he was making some shrewd guesses. "I suppose I might as well complete my explanation," he said shortly. "I didn't go into detail before since I felt that I didn't want anyone else to get involved. You'd better know now."

"Who is he?"

"That part I'll still keep to myself. I don't accuse any man until I can prove what I say."

"You're foolish," Marcy told him. "You're making it difficult for those of us who would like to help you."

"Sorry. Now let me tell it my way. Here's how I lost that supply train that there's been so much fuss about. I was on a scouting detail with eight men when I received a message from my company commander telling me to meet a supply train at a certain spot and convoy it to the advance base of the main column. I found the train easily enough, but the wagon boss handed me new orders, signed by the regimental adjutant. The train was to be turned over to a battalion of Texas volunteers.

"I saw no reason to question the second lot of orders so I obeyed them. I turned the outfit over to a squad of mounted irregulars who met me at the spot mentioned in the order. They spoke good English and I saw no reason to doubt them. Only when I rejoined my outfit after continuing the original scouting assignment did I learn that I had lost the train to a Mex guerrilla."

"Didn't you still have your order as evidence?"

"I had it — but no one could tell what it was. I'd swum my horse across the Rio Grande with the paper in my pants pocket. It was worthless — and no one had ever written such an order. Obviously they thought I had made up the whole story to clear myself of the charges that were being made against me."

"Didn't any of your men know about it?"

"No. I was handed the false message in confidence by the wagon boss. I guess you can see where this story is headed. That wagon boss is with this train now — and he has already made a couple of attempts to kill me. I'm guessing that it was one of his hired thugs who saw our bout with the Mormons last night."

Marcy grunted worriedly. "Maybe it was just coincidence that he passed the word to Burns — but maybe there's more. At any rate you have two enemies to watch now. Burns will be sore enough to give your other chum a bit of help if he can find a chance."

"A good reason why you should ignore me. You'll have plenty of your own troubles before this army gets out of the mess it's in."

"We'll forget that for the present. There's our headquarters just ahead. I might mention that Major

Pierce is likewise a pet dislike of Captain Burns. The major wasn't content to get his wife out of the baggage train; he told Burns face-to-face that he didn't want him poking his nose into personal affairs."

"I think I'll like Major Pierce," Spencer commented dryly.

They broke off the talk to ride in close to a camp which had been set up in the angle of two parked wagons. An officer in uniform seemed to be occupied with paper work on the seat of one of the wagons while an enlisted man busied himself at the fire. The cooking was being done by two women. Evidently there was no longer to be any concealment about their presence in the camp.

One of the women was a buxom red-haired matron who appeared brisk and efficient with her camp duties, her manner determinedly cheerful as she gossiped with the blonde girl. Miss Corliss was not saying much, but she did not appear to be troubled by her situation. Spencer wondered how she would react to his arrival.

Major Pierce jumped down from his perch to greet Marcy, and Spencer saw that he resembled Marcy in many ways. Even his informal salute hinted that dignity was for the major something to be shed at a moment's notice. Spencer half grunted his approval and then Marcy was introducing him.

He shook hands with the major and bowed a little stiffly to the red-haired woman. She was cordial and he decided that Ruth Corliss had fallen into good hands. Then he met the eyes of the blonde girl, fully aware that the others were watching curiously.

He knew that he was deliberately being perverse about it but still he made his voice very formal as he said, "I'm sorry to bring bad news, Miss Corliss, but I have to report that the two wagons in my train were burned last night by the Mormon cavalry. If they were contracted to the army in your own name, you will do well to make the proper legal claims as soon as possible. If they were leased to Callahan, he will undoubtedly enter the claims and make settlement with you."

She frowned a little as he spoke and he had the feeling that she was more concerned about his manner than the report of damage. Probably she already knew that her wagons were among those destroyed.

"Thank you," she said formally. "I placed all my business affairs in Mr. Callahan's hands. He did not feel that I should appear as an independent contractor any longer, so the wagons were under lease to him."

"Then you don't need to bother," Spencer assured her. "Callahan will take good care of everything. At least he has always done so in the past."

She looked away before murmuring, "He certainly seems to have been thorough in the arrangements that involved me. Thorough and imaginative!"

Spencer grinned, dropping the elaborate formality. "So I heard. I'd like to be close behind that miserable Irishman just about the time he starts to chuckle over the trick he played — and I'll bet he's done a piece of chuckling."

"When did you learn about it?" she asked suspiciously.

"When a lieutenant brought the word that Burns was on the warpath. I rode up along the line to see if there was anything I could do but you were already gone — and reported to be in good hands."

"Thanks to my friends here. Major Pierce is the person who first explained to me why so many people were calling me missus. He and Mrs. Pierce understood the situation at once and invited me to come here. It relieved the situation."

"And I, for one, am most disappointed," the redheaded Mrs. Pierce put in. "I thought I could detect romance in spite of what Ruth kept telling me, but now I must surrender. All you do is talk business. You might as well gather around and eat. We still have a bit of decent food so enjoy it before the Mormons steal any more of it from us."

Spencer asked one more question of Miss Corliss as they moved toward the cooking fire. "Any word of your sister?"

She shook her head. "Nothing direct. A scout named Cal Trent stopped here the other day. He seemed to know me and he made himself quite at home, not even introducing himself until he'd had supper. Then he told me rather abruptly that I should find some information at Fort Bridger. I didn't have any opportunity to ask questions; he simply faded out as soon as he said it."

"Sounds like Cal," Spencer told her. "Next time he's just as likely to sleep under a wagon all night. Maybe you can get a bit more information out of him — if he has any. I imagine he's merely passing on a rumor."

"How far is Fort Bridger from here?"

"About twenty miles."

"Then I should know something very soon."

"If Trent was right. I understand the scouts are working in that direction now, trying to see how much trouble the Mormons are preparing."

The conversation became general at that point, the two officers particularly showing a keen interest in what Spencer could tell them about the trail ahead. It was clear that both men were anticipating real trouble.

Spencer told them as concisely as possible, working out a sort of map on the ground with blanket rolls to represent ridges and cooking utensils as peaks. "We're about a hundred and fifty miles from Salt Lake by the shortest route," he explained. "That route runs through these gaps here. This is Echo Canyon. It's twenty-five miles long and built like a sluice box. If this man Lot Smith, who is reported to be the Mormon military commander, is as smart as I think he is, he'll fortify it. With a little work he can block it at any one of a dozen places — or he can throw up a few dams and put the whole thing under water."

"Isn't there a better trail?" Major Pierce asked.

"Not a better one. We could follow the eastern slope of the rim of the Great Basin to Soda Springs — about a hundred miles, I'd say — then follow the Bear River to the Roseaux. That would take us into Salt Lake Valley. Total distance would be some three hundred miles — and we can't afford that much extra travel. Winter is almost here."

"You know the country, Spencer," Pierce persisted. "What would you do if you had to make the choice?"

"I'd curse the men who put me into such a position by their crazy delays."

"We've already done that," Marcy cut in dryly. "What would you do after you stopped cursing?"

Spencer grimaced in recognition of the grim humor. "I'd fort up my wagons here with enough infantry to guard them well. Then I'd mount every available man on any animal that could carry them and send them at the double over the Soda Springs trail. With luck they could flank the Mormon militia and threaten Salt Lake. That ought to open the Echo Canyon route."

"What about the time element?"

"Bad. I don't offer it as a workable plan. It's just the best bet."

"Then you think the Mormons will defend Echo Canyon?"

"If they don't they're crazy — and so far they have played their cards very well."

"Would your plan take the army to Fort Bridger?" Miss Corliss asked.

"No." He made it brisk and short because there was no point in doing otherwise. It was a fact to be faced just as were other unpleasant facts like the threat of snow. No one argued.

CHAPTER TWELVE

The army remained idle throughout the following morning. There was plenty of activity in the camp as wagons continued to roll in with their guard detachments, but no advance order came from Colonel Alexander and the atmosphere of tension mounted until it affected both talk and movement. Men muttered uneasily or broke into senseless quarrels over nothing; platoon commanders and noncoms were kept busy all morning with the task of preventing open violence. On the march men had been too active and too tired to think much about their dangerous situation; in idleness they found the opportunity to worry — and to place the blame.

Just before noon, Lieutenant Bickford and the scout company rode in from the southwest and Spencer had his first look at the officer who had taken Marcy's place as commander of the irregulars. Bickford was a lean, hard-looking fellow, but somehow he did not appear to have the drive essential to such a post. His eyes were tired and a little troubled, but that was not to be wondered at. Many men looked that way this morning. What Spencer did not like was the way the lieutenant ignored his company as they approached Alexander's headquarters. A scout officer who did not have the knack of making himself a part of his command usually wasn't worth his salt.

Bickford remained with Colonel Alexander throughout the noon period and in early afternoon orderlies hurried through the camp to call a general council of all officers of and above the rank of company commander. At Marcy's insistence, Spencer attended, and his appearance caused some raised eyebrows but no open comments.

After a few preliminaries Alexander came to the point. He described the geography of the region in much the same terms Spencer had used on the previous evening, stressing the fact that a decision had to be reached immediately.

"You gentlemen know the situation, I think," he said quietly. "No provision has been made in our orders for conducting a war, but war has actually been declared by the Mormon leaders. The enemy has already struck a crippling blow at our supply trains and this morning they had the effrontery to place this ultimatum in the hands of Lieutenant Bickford."

He read from a crumpled paper which had been lying before him. "The unlawful force now threatening to invade the peace and quiet of Utah Territory is hereby warned against such illegal action. Already we have shown you your own helplessness and warning is issued that no stone will be left unturned to prevent entry into our land. It is ordered that you surrender all of your arms to the quartermaster of our army. If you comply with this demand you will be permitted to withdraw eastward as soon as the winter is over. Meanwhile your troops and other people will be supplied with the necessary food to maintain you through the cold season. Otherwise your people will certainly perish of the cold, your bodies left to rot in the mountains."

He waited for the angry murmur to subside and then added, "This is signed by Brigham Young himself. I suppose it requires no comment."

Major Pierce broke the silence. "I could think of a number of comments, Colonel, mostly profane, but I presume you want nothing but constructive suggestions."

Alexander permitted himself a fleeting smile. "I think that states the case for all of us, Major. That is why I have called this council. We must make our move quickly or be subject to the dangers our correspondent mentions so dramatically. Since there is no one in formal command I propose to assume that authority, in accordance with the best advice of this council. Major Burns, are you ready with your report on the state of the commissary?"

Burns looked surprised and uneasy. "It is ready, sir," he replied. "Do you want it in detail?"

"No. Only the essentials that will affect our situation now."

"Very well, sir." He swallowed hard. "We have five wagons of flour remaining, two wagons of bacon. There is a serious shortage of shoes and clothing."

Alexander did not waste time in recriminations. It was recognized that the bad judgment of the quartermaster officials had made it possible for the first raids to be so effective. "You understand the emergency, gentlemen. We must move at once — and we seem to have two alternatives. The direct route is still open beyond Fort Bridger. Our scouts report no fortifications in Echo Canyon, but there seems to be a strong belief that the canyon will be blocked or used as a site for an ambush. The alternate route is perhaps twice as long but not so susceptible to ambush or effective defense. May I have your opinions?"

Lieutenant Bickford spoke at once. "I recommend the direct route, sir. Personally, I discount the talk of ambush. My men report the trail open. That is enough for me."

That provoked a general expression of opinion and Colonel Alexander had to rap for order. An infantry captain spoke in support of Bickford's proposal and Marcy outlined the plan Spencer had suggested. No other scheme seemed feasible and the council boiled down to a rather hot debate on the two alternatives.

Spencer had hoped that Colonel Alexander would use his authority now that he had formally assumed it, but the officer temporized, searching for a compromise which would seem to avoid dissension among his officers.

"I think we understand each other," he said finally. "These are your orders. The entire command will move out at dawn tomorrow. We will take the route through Soda Springs and trust that the weather may be merciful. Unit commanders will please have everything ready for the movement as indicated."

It was clear that no one was satisfied by the compromise, but military rule permitted no further dispute. Marcy made no comment until they were clear of the dispersing council. Then he asked dryly, "Do you think we'll get through?"

Spencer shook his head. "I'm sure we won't. A mounted force traveling light might have had a chance. Wagons will never have time."

During the afternoon Spencer wandered through the crowded camp. The past few weeks had permitted him scant opportunity to think about the factors which had brought him into this situation, but now he took steps to locate the Donnel train. The very confusion of the expedition would play into Donnel's hands and Spencer knew that he had to be prepared. His own situation was almost like that of the floundering army — he could not strike any effective blow in his own behalf. All he could do was to risk an exposed position in the hopes that his chance would come.

After supper Spencer went with Marcy to Major Pierce's wagon. He did not contemplate the evening with any great joy. There was always a certain amount of pleasure to be anticipated from the presence of Ruth Corliss, but he knew that her problem was as unhappy as his own.

They found Cal Trent enjoying the Pierce hospitality. The ragged old scout was cleaning up a dish of stew, a fair portion of it already decorating his disreputable whiskers. Evidently he had been entertaining them with stories of his trapping experiences, for his listeners seemed amused even though a little puzzled by him. He looked up once at Spencer, grinned in what seemed like relief, and then returned to his supper.

Miss Corliss came across quickly, frowning a little as she murmured to Spencer, "I don't know what this man wants. He came here and invited himself to supper. Now he talks endlessly but won't answer questions."

"Let me handle him," Spencer told her. "I think I know what this might mean."

He let a bit of preliminary small talk drift around the fire and then remarked, "I didn't see you with the other scouts today, Cal. Been looking around a bit?"

"Yep. Mormons gittin' mighty active up Echo Canyon. Looks like they figger to fight it out there."

"How far up?"

"Can't tell. Mebbe ten miles." He made an elaborate ceremony of scrubbing out his pannikin and placing it with the other utensils. Then he shot a sidelong glance at the girl and muttered, "I looked around a bit at Bridger."

"Looking for anything special?" Spencer encouraged.

"Yep. Like Anvil told me. The lady's lookin' fer somethin'."

"Find it?"

Again there was a flat silence. Finally Trent shrugged slightly and blurted out, "Got some grave markers there. One of 'em has got the name of Anne Corliss on it."

Then he slipped out of the firelight so swiftly that his disappearance seemed almost ghostly.

Again there was a tense silence. Spencer knew that the others were thinking as he thought. A girl had come across five thousand miles of ocean and rough trails to have this fatal news thrown at her abruptly in a beleaguered camp.

She took it almost stoically, her voice small but calm as she said, "Now I know. There can be no doubt now." Her tone indicated that she had long ago given up any real hope. Verification had been almost a relief.

"Now you must return east," Mrs. Pierce told her, obviously trying to make practical matters cover the emotional upset. "There will be empty wagons going back, I'm sure."

"I'm afraid not," Captain Marcy said. "Today's orders prohibit any further return movements. All animals are to remain with the expedition. Empty wagons will be abandoned. We're badly short of stock, both edible and draft."

"It's better to stick with the army," Spencer added. "Utah is three hundred miles; Kansas is a thousand. If the worst comes to the worst it's better to be snowed in with friends than along the trail somewhere."

"You think that will happen?" the girl asked quietly.

"I wouldn't bet against it."

The following morning the army began its march, toiling along Ham's Fork and cutting a road through the thickets of greasewood and wild sage so that the baggage wagons could find a passage. Troop units were now interspersed with wagon trains so that no part of the column was unguarded, but it was slow, back-breaking work for the men breaking trail. They made little progress and when the advance guard made camp that night many wagons were still at the original encampment. Once more the line was strung out in vulnerable fashion and Colonel Alexander made shift to offset the lack of cavalry cover. Two companies of the Fifth were mounted on mules taken from the baggage train to patrol the entire line as dragoons might have done.

They were not a very military-looking unit, but they proved their worth the next day. The Mormons evidently had received word of this new march, for their raiding parties appeared all along the line, keeping just out of rifle-shot as they watched for some opportunity to cut off wagons or stampede the stock. The mule-mounted infantrymen were no match for the wild-riding Mormon horsemen, but they managed to prevent any serious raids against the train. Spencer rode with Marcy most of the time, silently disgruntled at the role the troops were forced to play.

On several occasions he passed the Donnel wagons and on the second trip he saw Major Burns talking to Donnel. The two men studied him silently as he passed and he knew they were discussing him. He wondered how much talking Donnel might do, but he realized that it did not matter very much. The important point was to remember that the pair had been together.

For three days the army made painfully slow progress, the Mormon riders always hovering on the flanks, and the days became more and more gray as the cold intensified. Nor was there any consolation for Spencer in being able to visit Ruth Corliss. The girl had kept strictly to her wagon since getting the news about her sister's fate. She was not making any show of her troubles, but she was in no mood for conversation.

That night the Mormon cavalry ran off eight hundred head of cattle from the rear of the train, skillfully evading the mule dragoons who tried too late to stop them. As soon as the news reached him, Spencer went out with some of Bickford's scouts. There might be a chance of intercepting the stolen herd, so every effort was to be made. For an army already short of rations, the loss would be staggering.

The scouts spent the night in the mountains, turning back just before dawn when it became certain that they had not guessed correctly as to the direction the raiders would take. A mile short of the fork they met a party of Marcy's men, who were elated at having captured two prisoners. The Mormons were correspondingly disgusted at having been taken prisoner by what they disdainfully called "jackass cavalry."

"I like to hear 'em holler," a grinning sergeant laughed. "It's the fust time we've had anything to crow about on our side. One of 'em's a major and the other feller's his adjutant. They had some right important-lookin' papers that I figger Cap'n Marcy's gonna be right interested in."

Spencer went along with the soldiers, curious to see what the papers might reveal. Captain Marcy examined them without delay but they did not tell much. Mostly they were orders issued by General Wells, commander of the Nauvoo Legion. They directed the various raiding parties to burn the country before the invaders, to stage continuous night attacks which would keep the weary troops from resting, to stampede animals and set fire to wagons whenever the opportunity presented itself, to blockade the road by falling trees, to destroy fords and ferries — but to take no life.

"Not much new," Marcy commented. "They've been doing just that."

"But now we know we may expect more of it," Spencer said. "The chance of getting through Echo Canyon would have been scant even if no fortifications showed there."

"We'll simply push on," Marcy declared. "Smith's men should come up within a day or two. Some of them are supposed to be well mounted."

The prediction proved too optimistic. Smith had sent word that he would use a cutoff which had been suggested to him but when the train reached rendezvous Smith's units had not yet arrived. The train could do nothing but push on.

On the following morning they could not even do that. A whirling snowstorm blanketed the camp at daylight and by the time breakfast was over travel conditions were next to impossible. Some of the men were sent out to clear the trail but no wagons were moved. By midmorning the snow was a foot deep on the level and the work parties were recalled. Colonel Alexander called a meeting of company officers and scouts.

There was nothing for the council to decide. Just as it went into session a snow-crusted courier floundered into camp with lengthy orders from the east, forwarded from Colonel Smith's belated force. General Harney had finally been replaced as commander of the expedition. Colonel Albert Sidney Johnston of the Second Cavalry had been appointed his successor and Colonel Johnston was now hurrying to his post, sending orders ahead of him for the army to concentrate on Black's Fork, only a few miles beyond the old camp on Ham's Fork. Colonel Johnston had already overtaken Colonel Smith and the Tenth Infantry units and their combined forces now totaled some three hundred men, only a handful of whom were dragoons. The Second Dragoons had been retained in Kansas by Governor Walker and General Harney.

After the first flush of excitement it was not such wonderful news. "Lord knows we need a commander," Marcy said in an aside to Spencer, "but we need dragoons worse. I wonder if this man Johnston knows what he's doing."

"Sounds like it," Spencer muttered. "He's going to close in on Fort Bridger for winter headquarters, I imagine. That makes better sense than to drag this wagon train around the way we're doing."

Few seemed to feel that way about it. The very business of turning back hurt the morale of the army and it was a dejected column which reversed itself the next day and began to work back through the snow toward the old camp on Ham's Fork. Wagons slipped and slid as the snow froze on the rocky trail that had been so laboriously cleared. Firewood for each camp had to be brought in from a distance by forage parties, everything along the line of march having been cleared off on the way upstream. Men stumbled and fell in the winter wilderness. Every night the Mormons raided diligently, keeping the camps in a perpetual uproar. For men who could not sleep at night the snow-covered trail was a complete horror in daylight. With the temperature at zero, weariness was beginning to take its toll.

The nightmare march lasted a fortnight, but on November 2, in the middle of another blizzard, the first wagons of the train went into camp at the appointed spot on Black's Fork. The army had been under a constant strain for nearly a month and many of the wagons were still getting through the old camp on Ham's Fork. For all practical purposes the expedition was exactly where it had been a month earlier.

Physically the army was definitely behind its status of the earlier camp. Draft animals were virtually walking skeletons; the month of labor had completed the job of breaking them down. The stock had been sacrificed for a gain of nothing.

Spencer traveled close to the Pierce wagon during most of the final week of the march, leaving most of the scouting to the men who were supposed to do it. Marcy made the suggestion in the first place, feeling that Spencer might help Ruth Corliss break out of her melancholy, and Spencer made no objections. It gave him an opportunity to talk a little with her, hopeful that closer relations might make her forget that she had once resented his refusal to help. After a week he could not be sure that he had made much progress. She was cordial enough but no more than decency required.

Her manner seemed to accept him as a sort of partner in trouble, but he could not imagine that there was any more to it than that.

The feeling left him so disgruntled that he made it a point not to remain long at the Pierce camp in the evenings. Once he had seen that the two women were comfortable for the night, he slipped away, joining either a scout group or some unit of the Fifth, whichever proved closer. It was partly this unhappy preoccupation and partly weariness which made him relax his vigilance one evening. He was striding along through the frozen slush toward a tiny fire which marked the camp of a guard platoon when suddenly a crunch of snow crust warned of a movement at his back. He swung to meet what he realized would be an assualt, but the moment of carelessness had lasted a trifle too long. There was time for him to see two hulking forms hurling themselves upon him and then he went down under a flurry of vicious blows. Pain racked him from several places at once as he fought to ward them off — then he knew no more.

CHAPTER THIRTEEN

Consciousness came back gradually. Spencer knew that he was between blankets and in a covered wagon, but for a long time he did not bother to wonder what blankets or whose wagon. After some minutes of dim awareness he realized that he was bandaged in several places and sore in many others. What seemed to be daylight came through gaps in the canvas, but he found trouble in focusing his eyes.

While he was trying to piece it all together, the canvas flap opened and a grotesque but familiar figure appeared. It was certainly Ruth Corliss, but dim vision did tricks with the ice on her hood and shoulders. She looked thoroughly miserable and he realized guiltily that she had been out in the storm because he was occupying her place in the wagon.

"Howdy," he said, his voice sounding thin and a bit ridiculous in his own ears. "How's the weather out there?"

"I'm glad you have awakened," she said quickly, climbing into the wagon and drawing the flaps against the driving sleet. "We have been terribly worried." Then she forced a smile and added, "The weather is lovely — if you care to breathe ice."

He tried to sit up but was promptly halted by the girl's quick hand and his own painful helplessness. One of his arms didn't seem to work at all and after one effort he did not need her anxious, "Lie quietly, please. You must not exert yourself."

He fought the waves of blackness for what seemed like a long time, but when the pain subsided his head seemed clearer. "What happened to me?" he asked.

"Later," she said. "Can you swallow some broth? Captain Yates, the Tenth's regimental surgeon, left orders that you were to have nourishment as quickly as possible."

"How long ago was that? I feel as though I hadn't eaten for a week."

"Almost three days," she informed him. "Be quiet now and I'll get the broth. I'm afraid it is made from a deceased draft ox, but it is the best we have to offer."

"Better bring a cut of the ox." He tried to sound better than he felt.

She went out into the storm again, returning quickly with a mess tin that steamed invitingly in the cold air. Removing the sleet-crusted hood, she shook the snow from her cape and settled beside him to help him with the broth, her smile a little stronger now. He decided that she was a very pretty girl, even with a red nose.

The hot soup brought back some of his energy and a good measure of his spirits. "Now tell me what happened to me," he urged.

"Are you sure you feel well enough to talk?"

His twisted grin hurt but it was worth it to get the answering smile. "I'll listen," he said. "You do the talking."

"Gittin' uppity already," she frowned, her voice a good imitation of the Cal Trent drawl. "So I'll tell you in detail. Maybe that will take some of the ginger out of you. First, there is a gash on the side of your head. Second, a broken nose with two black eyes to set it off. Third, a shoulder that was dislocated but which is now strapped up tightly. I won't make any inventory of the assorted cuts and bruises. If I may quote Mr. Trent once more, 'Mister, yo're a mess!' "

"You sound pretty cheerful about it," he commented. "Sounds like you think I got what I deserved — maybe because I refused to handle your wagons for you."

"You could think of it that way," she told him airily. "Actually I am following Captain Yates' instructions. The cheerful bedside manner, he calls it."

"Thanks."

"Don't be cross. I might as well admit that I'm so relieved that I can't help sounding a little foolish."

"Thanks again. This time I mean it."

"You had better try to get some sleep now," she said hastily.

"After three days of it? What I need is to know who provided me with all these gory details you seemed to delight in listing. I remember a couple of men jumping me along the trail but — you take it from there."

"I'm afraid I can tell you nothing. All I know is that two men from Captain Marcy's company brought you here. They said they heard the sound of a fight and hurried to the scene. They found you in the snow and they believed that two men had run away as they approached. Captain Marcy has been investigating, but I think you understand how useless it would be. Nothing could be learned. Everyone has been much too busy staying alive."

"Then the army has been having more troubles?"

"Many more. We are gathered together on Black's Fork now but the added strength of Colonel Johnston's escort has not put any stop to Mormon raiding. Not that they can do much harm now; we are losing animals by starvation and freezing much faster than raiders can steal them. The train is completely out of forage."

Spencer did not say anything more for quite a while. Obviously the expedition was in a serious predicament. Short of food, short of most supplies, out of forage, animals dying off from starvation — and still nearly 150 miles from Salt Lake. When he let his thoughts get to the surface again it was to ask, "Have you heard anything about the Mormons blocking Echo Canyon?"

"It has been done, I understand."

"What kind of advance does this Colonel Johnston plan?"

"No one seems to know exactly. There is a rumor that the army will push on to Fort Bridger. No one talks about what the wagon train will do. Maybe we'll stay right here."

"Easy," he warned. "You're letting yourself sound pretty glum."

"I feel that way."

"Come now!" he chided. "Remember that cheerful bedside manner."

"A little of it at a time is all I can muster. You might as well understand that the army's situation is desperate."

An hour later Captain Marcy came into the wagon. "I hear you're coming around, Spencer," he greeted. "I certainly hope so. We'll be moving soon and the bumping of the wagon won't make you feel any better."

"How far this time?"

"Only a short distance. Colonel Johnston has found a sheltered spot about two miles this side of Fort Bridger. If our animals can make it, we'll go into winter quarters there."

"I know the spot. It'll do."

Marcy nodded. "I've been busy with another matter, Spencer, and I hope you won't think I'm prying into your affairs. A little over a week ago Colonel Alexander told me that he had information about your past. When I told him the truth of it he admitted that his knowledge had come from Captain Burns. Burns had gone out of his way to give him another warning about you."

"Nice of him," Spencer muttered.

"And suspicious. I wanted to know how Burns had gotten his ideas. So I set Sergeant Peace on the captain. Do you know Gabe Peace?"

"Not by name."

"He's the lanky tobacco-chewing rascal who captured those two Mormons. A good man, Spencer. I'd trust him with anything. Anyway, he came up with a quick answer. Burns was visiting a freighter named Catlett."

"The name was Donnel on the Mexican border," Spencer said dryly. "This man Peace must be a good spy. Too bad he didn't go to Salt Lake in place of Van Vliet. You might have gotten a true report instead of the one that came in."

"Forget Salt Lake. Is this man Catlett — or Donnel — the one you have been trying to trap?"

"He's the lad. Some day — if he doesn't kill me first, I hope to prove that he had a hand in giving me a forged order after planning to have the wagon picked off by a guerrilla leader named Garcia. As long as we are now naming names you might as well have the whole thing."

"I thought it would be something like that. To get on with the story, I told Peace to keep a man or two in sight of Catlett's outfit all the time. They report that two men left the camp on the evening you were attacked. When they returned they went directly to the boss, evidently reporting something. And one of them had a bloody nose."

Spencer grinned even though it hurt. "Now I feel better," he declared. "I didn't think I'd done any kind of job of defending myself."

Marcy shook off the interruption. "The time fits exactly with the attack upon you. Then, on the following morning before the train moved, Catlett left his wagons and was gone perhaps a half hour. When he returned there was quite a row. One of Peace's men heard his cussing out the pair who had been away from camp, calling them blundering idiots and similar fine terms. It seems like a fair bet that he had just learned of their failure to kill you."

"That's army for you," Spencer sighed. "All this show of brains in the lower ranks. I wonder why they never have any generals that smart?"

"Mention that to Sergeant Peace the first time you see him," Marcy suggested with a chuckle. "With sentiments like that you'll be his friend for life. Now stop trying to be funny and tell me what you propose to do about this Catlett or Donnel or whatever you call him."

"I'll keep on waiting. There isn't anything else to do. I've got to make him show his hand if I'm to gain anything. It won't do to take a return smack at him — when and if I'm physically able. I've got to trap him into making the statement I must have. Nothing else counts."

"Do you have any plans?"

"No. That has been the worst of it all along. I can't plan a thing. All I can do is watch for an opportunity and hope I'll get it before he gets me."

"A forlorn hope, I'd call it."

"Maybe. But it's the only play I have."

"One other thing," Marcy said after a brief pause. "I took the liberty to talk this over with Miss Corliss. I hoped that she might be able to help me with my investigations. When I discovered that she knew nothing about your affairs, I felt a bit guilty to have talked. I thought you should know."

"No objection," Spencer said quickly. "I'm grateful that you were interested. Perhaps it will be better that she knows. I seem to be pretty much dependent upon her charity just now."

"Not a bad situation at that," Marcy said with a grin. "Many a man would be willing to trade places with you, contusions and all."

The next morning the train began a new movement, a slow, painful inching forward that was at times no movement at all. Every wagon was short of draft animals and the miserable creatures that could be put into harness were almost without strength. Only when men put shoulders to the wheels did the train make any progress through the continuing sleet storm. The jolting sent Spencer back into brief spells of blackness and at the end of the day he was not even interested in the report that less than two miles had been covered.

He was never entirely clear about the happenings of the next day or two. When he was awake he was conscious of little but discomfort. Once in a while he knew that Ruth Corliss was with him and then the pain did not seem so bad. He had fallen in love with her, he supposed with a curious sense of detachment. The idea was interesting but he didn't know just what could be done about it. Certainly this man Spencer — whom he seemed to know as a sort of familiar stranger — was no fellow to be marrying.

On the third day of the march, the fog cleared a little and he was able to sit up long enough to look out upon the world of white through which the army was forcing itself. He recalled reading a description of Napoleon's retreat from Moscow and it seemed probable that here was an American duplicate. A snowy wilderness had trapped a bewildered, helpless army, pinning it down while its enemies harassed it. His mood was not lightened when he realized that he was one of the most helpless members of the impotent expedition. His own vague plans had been blocked quite as effectively as winter and the Mormon cavalry had blocked this army.

During the third day's march Miss Corliss came into the wagon with him at every halt, ostensibly to see that he needed nothing, but really, he thought, because she was cold. Still she refused to ride, recognizing the necessity for saving the worn-out oxen. She did not talk very much at any time and Spencer believed that he knew why. The army was slowly but steadily moving toward Fort Bridger. She must be thinking about what she expected to see there. For her the march was a reopening of the old wound.

The next day the surgeon stopped to see him, announcing cheerfully that the worst was over. The blow on the head had been the most serious injury, but the concussion seemed to have run its course. Proper rest and a little extra care for the injured shoulder would take care of everything.

To Spencer that meant getting out of the wagon and ceasing to be a burden to other people, but he quickly met unanimous opposition. Major Pierce and Captain Marcy joined with the two women in bullying him pleasantly but definitely. He was to stay where he was. There was not going to be any arguments about it. "It'll be easier that way," Marcy explained. "My men have their orders to keep you in sight. Don't make it hard for them."

He obeyed for a week, a week spent in the snows with the wagon train inching its painful way toward Fort Bridger. Only when Spencer left the cover of the wagon did he realize how slow that progress was. In eleven days the train had done approximately twenty-five miles.

The interval did something for Ruth Corliss, however. She seemed to have recovered some of her spirits and spent hours with Spencer, discussing his problem. He found it pleasant to know that someone was interested and they worked over several schemes calculated to force a statement out of Curt Donnel, none of which ever sounded very smart on second examination. It began to appear that everything connected with this expedition had been contaminated with the same brand of futility. The girl's efforts had led to nothing except a knowledge of tragedy. Spencer had succeeded in absolutely nothing. The army was trapped in a position that was both futile and desperate.

They finally arrived at the new camp on the sixteenth of November after covering thirty miles in two weeks. Now the prospect seemed a little brighter. Colonel Johnston had evidently put some vigor into the command and the new camp was being set up with energy and intelligence. No permanent huts were being constructed, the commander apparently hoping that this would not be the end of the march, but otherwise preparations were being made for the comfort and safety of the men who would be living here. Some of the new-type tents, built along the lines of the Indian wigwam, were going up in orderly lines to supplement the wagons which would also be used for shelters. Slaughterhouses were already in operation to butcher the exhausted draft animals in place of the stock which had been run off by Indians and Mormons.

The camp site was the one Spencer had supposed earlier. It occupied a stretch of flatland along Black's Fork nearly a mile in length and varying from three to six hundred yards wide. The stream flowed along one side, providing ample water supplies, while the other flank was protected by a series of high, almost perpendicular, cliffs. The position offered good protection against weather and raiders, but it was lacking in any kind of forage. Colonel Johnston recognized that fact immediately and ordered all stock not destined for the slaughter pits to be transferred to a spot some thirty-five miles south on Henry's Fork. A second camp was established there for the troops of the Tenth who were to act as guards.

On Black's Fork the various units were assigned locations in a manner that would offer the best protection against raiders. The Fifth Infantry camped at the southeastern end, closest to Fort Bridger. At the northern end several units of the Tenth, along with the artillery company, formed a barrier against attack. In between were the wagon divisions.

It was this center which was now becoming a real problem. Many of the teamsters were little better than outlaws and with this sudden shift to idleness their presence became a constant danger. Most of them blamed the army for the position in which they found themselves and they made no secret of the fact that they did not propose to be bound by military rules. Even before the camp was set up there was much looting and several fatal fights. To Spencer this represented a new danger, not only to himself but to the women who were in the camp. He saw to it that Major Pierce placed his wagons squarely in the center of the Fifth's camp, but beyond that he could do little. With several months of winter in prospect the outlook was not happy.

CHAPTER FOURTEEN

In spite of the background of worry, Spencer spent a week of something that was almost happiness. By the time camp arrangements were completed he was getting around quite capably and it suited him well enough that Marcy should give him the responsibility of looking after the Pierce wagons. He and Ruth Corliss were on a first name basis now, a sort of comradeship having sprung up between them which was none the less real for its uncertainty of origin. He was grateful for the way she had taken care of him, but his feelings went deeper than that. He could only hope that her easy cordiality had similar backgrounds.

On the nineteenth of November Colonel Johnston began the recruiting of an irregular unit to be used as scouts and hunters. Meat for the winter camp could be supplemented by wild game and it seemed like a good idea to get men into the hills without delay. At the same time the formation of a scout company would provide occupation for some of the idle teamsters who were causing daily riots. Large numbers of them had grimly started a march eastward, risking the wintry weather, but the camp still was full of idle, roistering, irresponsible riffraff.

On that same day Spencer made his first trip away from the wagon which had been his home for nearly three weeks. He was curious about the make-up of the camp, but mostly he wanted to see what was happening around the Donnel wickiups. That part was not reassuring. None of Donnel's crew had left for Kansas and none of them had joined the new company. That hinted at some sort of plan, a plan which Spencer guessed would mean trouble for himself.

Colonel Cooke and the Second Dragoons arrived late the following day. They were a woebegone-looking group of troopers and Spencer noted that the remount men were bringing almost no extra horses. He knew what it meant even before he heard the report that they had lost almost a third of their entire stock since leaving South Pass. Cold and hunger had killed horses even though the riders had discarded the bulk of their equipment to lighten the loads.

"Ever since a month before we left Leavenworth," Marcy grumbled, "we've been waiting for the dragoons to join us. Finally they're here, now that we don't have any particular need for them. And what shape are they in? Exhausted! Not a man in the lot will be fit for service this month — and not a horse will live over the winter unless we're luckier than we can hope."

"I hope Governor Walker and General Harney got some good out of them in Kansas," Major Pierce commented grimly. "They certainly wrecked this expedition by holding them back there."

It was soon known throughout the camp that the dragoons had escorted some of the territorial officials being sent to Utah in replacement of the men the Mormons had driven out. Governor Cumming, slated to displace Brigham Young as governor of Utah, had finally decided to make the trip, after playing politics for extra pay until the last moment. The general opinion was that he would be just the man to make the Mormons even more resentful of Federal treatment of them. Most of the lesser officials were of much the some stamp although Judge Eckels was considered to be both honest and efficient, something which could not be said for most of the political hacks who had been sent to Salt Lake. For the present their arrival only complicated camp problems.

The cold abated suddenly that night and by morning much of the snow had turned to a dirty gray slush which kept everyone idle except for necessary chores. After a couple of very unpleasant days the ground was clear in many places. Spencer seized the opportunity to secure a reasonably fit horse for Ruth Corliss and take her on a brief trip to Fort Bridger. This seemed the proper thing to do. Once it was accomplished, he knew, the girl would be able to settle down.

The trip was not at all private. Men on forage details were constantly in sight as they covered the two miles to the old trading post. But Ruth kept her spirits up and proved a cheerful and charming companion. She seemed to have adjusted herself already to a realization of her sister's death. This trip would have a sort of sentimental purpose but nothing more.

They found the fort in ruins, its two black stone walls rising where the Mormons had fired the place.

Actually the Mormons had attempted to set fire to the entire valley, but the green willows and cottonwoods had failed to burn, a fact which was now being turned to account as men toiled to cut firewood while others began the rebuilding of the old fortifications. Bridger could serve as a defensible supply depot and Colonel Johnston had already moved to make it such.

"Too bad we didn't have this man Johnston and the dragoons from the beginning," Spencer said. "We'd be in Salt Lake now."

"We would if we'd started soon enough," Ruth added in a low voice. It seemed certain that she was thinking of another expedition that had been hamstrung by delays and poor leadership.

They did not remain long at Fort Bridger. An inspection of the forlorn little cemetery soon disclosed a cottonwood cross with a name and date scratched on it. The name was Anne Corliss and the date was significantly vague — 1857. Perhaps the girl had lived past the end of the year. Perhaps not.

Spencer and Ruth Corliss were silent as they rode slowly back along the fork past the newly erected tents of the civil officials. The waters of the stream, swollen by melting snow, rippled noisily over a stony bed. Axes rang among the willows. Men shouted here and there as they worked to prepare for the ordeal ahead. The screen was bleak but not any more bleak than the silence of Spencer and the girl. If either of them had known any doubts as to the hardships ahead, they were fully aware of them now.

The tension was broken a little when they returned to find Captain Marcy at the Pierce camp. He had news. Colonel Johnston was thinking ahead. An inventory of food supplies had been taken and it was calculated that the camp could survive until the following spring if rations were cut immediately. Many items were in short supply, largely due to the Morman raids, but the worst problem was meat. To offset that lack a force was being dispatched to New Mexico immediately. They were to return as quickly as possible with beef cattle so that the camp would be supplied by early spring. Meanwhile the butchering of draft animals would go on and that supply would be supplemented by whatever the hunters could bring in.

"Burns caught it," Marcy said with grim satisfaction. "The colonel has been saying plenty about the way the trains were loaded. We're short of food, practically shoeless, and utterly bankrupt so far as clothing is concerned."

"Don't forget our long supplies," Major Pierce put in wryly. "Lots of kettles for boiling brine — out of Salt Lake, I presume — a thousand leather neckstocks, three thousand empty bedsacks with no straw! It really took brains to outfit this expedition!"

Marcy interrupted the tirade, speaking soberly to Spencer. "I'm to command the force Colonel Johnston is sending to Taos. Lieutenant Bickford reported that the journey could not be made. Evidently his scouts agree with him because I have persuaded only two of them to go with me. Trent and Allen. The rest of the force will be drawn from my jackass cavalry. They don't know enough about the danger to play sick." He caught Spencer's frown and added quickly, "I'm not referring to you there, Dan. You're not only unfit to travel but I think you should remain here for other reasons."

"I'm fit," Spencer asserted. "You'd better take me along. I don't know much about Allen but I do know that Cal Trent is not too well versed in this part of the country."

"We'll get through. Just tell us what is the best route to take."

"At this time of year there is no best route. Just seven hundred miles of mountains without trails. I could find my way, but I'm not too sure of any other man in the expedition."

"Sorry." Marcy was definite now. "I have orders on that subject. Colonel Johnston has heard the rumors about you and he's not the man to take unnecessary chances. He's aware that we are in danger of being intercepted and he proposes to run no risks with a man who is rumored to be friendly with the enemy. You'll find a guard at your heels until we are well clear of this region. Sorry to put it to you like that, but you might as well know."

Major Pierce added, "You might as well know also that Captain Marcy is risking his own reputation to tell you this."

"I can understand." Spencer was finding it difficult to hide the bitterness in his voice even though he realized that Colonel Johnston was in no position to investigate the matter. As a commanding officer sending men into a dangerous mission, he could do nothing else.

"This is all strictly confidential," Marcy said, trying to get past the awkward spot. "We'll slip out of camp as quietly as possible and move over to Henry's Fork for the best mounts. After that we'll probably hit the Green and follow it to the junction with the Colorado. I'm told it's the best way."

"Either way is a gamble," Spencer told him. "You might save a bit of hard travel if you were to strike east and follow the eastern slopes of the Rockies — along past Pike's Peak and Long's Peak."

"Trent mentioned that but he feels he can find his way better if we follow the river."

Spencer shrugged. "It's an idea. Incidentally, when you're down in the Taos region see if you can pick up any gossip about a Mex named Garcia. You know the one I mean. If he operates around Santa Fe he'll probably be known at Taos. I'd be interested."

"I had it in mind," Marcy said quietly. "Now that he has nothing to fear from our government he might be willing to talk. Meanwhile, keep an eye on Donnel. He didn't miss far on his last try."

"I'll keep my eyes open. I'll be safer than you will, I imagine."

Marcy's smile was grim. "Incidentally, I have given orders for Sergeant Peace to handle the guard that has been set on you. He will stay with you day and night until my detachment is in the clear. Don't make it too difficult for him."

"We'll get along," Spencer promised. "You'll remember that the sergeant and I are supposed to have some undignified ideas in common."

"They're thick as thieves," Pierce broke in. "I've seen them together several times and my opinion is that they'll be running the camp before the winter's over."

"I figured on that." Marcy laughed, apparently glad to have the solemnity taken out of the talk. "Peace has his orders. If he's in doubt about anything, he is to ask Spencer. Otherwise he's on his own; my platoon commanders are instructed that he is on detached service and will take orders from Major Pierce."

"Sorry I'm not going with you," Spencer said quietly. "I'd like to serve under a man who lets his head do him some good in spite of all the red tape."

They ended the meeting there, shaking hands all around. Then Captain Marcy moved away without looking back. Spencer was left with feelings he could not quite analyze. In an army that had been notably inefficient Marcy had come to represent something substantial. And he was a good friend. It wasn't easy to see him go, knowing that he might never get through.

They were silent for several minutes. Then Major Pierce said briefly. "Better take the sergeant into your confidence, Spencer. It'll make matters easier all around." Then he too was gone.

That evening the atmosphere around the Pierce camp was one of somewhat strained jollity. Sergeant Peace had arrived with his bedroll and was making himself quite at home except for a little awkwardness at the moments when he had occasion to converse with Major Pierce.

Ruth Corliss and Mrs. Pierce kept the talk going, discussing the plans for the winter. Both professed to feel somewhat relieved that the army had finally achieved some stability. Instead of the endless, aimless traveling there was now a definite program to work on with some certainty that their efforts would not be in vain. Ruth was especially cheerful. She made it clear that henceforth she intended to consider this whole thing as an adventure to be experienced with as much enjoyment as possible.

"I hope you'll keep on thinking this way," Spencer told them after a time. "I'm quite aware that you're talking to make me forget the grumps I've got — but it's still good to hear you. Just keep it on that basis and the winter won't be half as bad as we might expect."

Ruth looked disappointed. "You're a mean man," she said. "We can't even try to cheer you up without having you tell us exactly what we're doing. That takes all the fun out of it."

"Not for me. I've very grateful that you'll set aside your own troubles in an attempt to make me forget mine. I don't remember ever having friends who would do that for me."

"Misery loves company," Sergeant Peace quoted dryly. "I'm cold."

That brought the talk back to a banter level and the evening passed happily enough. Only toward the end did Spencer have an opportunity to talk with Ruth alone.

"I'm glad you're remaining with us," she said quietly as she started to climb into her wagon. "I feel safer with you here. You always seem to know what to do."

"That's very flattering to a man who seems to have made a complete mess of everything — and it's dangerous talk."

"Dangerous? Why?"

"Because I'm likely to take it seriously. Suppose I should try to make you think that you needed me around all the time?"

She looked away into space as though considering the matter with some care. "I try to be reasonable," she said softly. "A reasonable person never refuses to hear a good argument."

He reached out a hand toward her, but she slipped away, a new note in her voice as she whispered, "With a whole winter ahead of us, I'll be expecting you to come up with some very fine arguments." Then she disappeared into the wagon.

Spencer smiled happily and a little quizzically, his thoughts divided between a sense of excitement and one of frustration. For the third time in recent hours he had been deprived of an answer. First Marcy, then Major Pierce, and now Ruth. Each one had gotten in a final word and slipped away hastily. Then he chuckled aloud. Somehow he didn't object at all to the sense of incompleteness in this final instance. It gave a man something to look forward to.

CHAPTER FIFTEEN

The thermometer registered a degree below zero when Spencer rolled out next morning. He and Sergeant Peace had set up sleeping quarters under Ruth's wagon, a tarpaulin from wheel to wheel making a rather decent shelter. Before going to sleep he had taken pains to make sure that his new ally understood the situation clearly and when he opened his eyes he had a feeling of general satisfaction. For the moment nothing seemed to require immediate attention. He did not even think about Curt Donnel. Maybe running him down wouldn't be worth the trouble after all.

By noon the temperature had dropped another ten degrees and the business of the day became mostly a matter of preparing for cold. No one seemed to mind. Mrs. Pierce had formed a sort of alliance with Sergeant Peace and they amused themselves with sly remarks about Spencer and Ruth. Since neither of the targets of the humor objected in the least, it made for a pleasant sort of day. For a group of people ambushed by winter and a hostile army they were doing rather well.

At noon one of Marcy's infantrymen came in with a report for Sergeant Peace. The sergeant met him a little distance from the camp and returned quickly. "One o' the boys watchin' Donnel's outfit," he told Spencer. "Cap'n Burns popped in about an hour ago and it looks like somethin's doin' there. They're packin' up."

That put an end to the easy air of the day. Spencer wanted to have a look for himself, but before they could decide on a movement Major Pierce returned from headquarters.

"There's a bit of information you might be interested in, Spencer," he announced. "Three of Donnel's men just came in to enlist in Colonel Johnston's new militia company. They say that the rest of their outfit is heading back to Kansas."

"I didn't think any eastward moves were being made now."

"Maybe I forgot to tell you. We had another little note from the Mormons yesterday. They warn us that they now have three thousand men surrounding this camp and that they propose to harass us all winter if we remain. At the same time they offer safe conduct to any units that will go back east. Several groups of teamsters are talking of making the effort, even though it now seems hopeless."

"What about Donnel himself?"

"I don't know. His men seemed a little evasive on that score."

"Captain Burns talked to him not long ago. Do you suppose it has anything to do with this sudden decision?"

"I don't know. Maybe you'd better take steps to find out."

It didn't take Spencer and Sergeant Peace long to discover that the Donnel camp had been abandoned with great dispatch. The wagons had been turned over to a noncom of the Quarter-master's Corps, but the man seemed to know nothing about them. His orders from Captain Burns had simply been to prevent looting until the government stores could be placed under regular supervision. He had not even seen the earlier occupants of the camp.

"We'll make a scout first thing in the morning," Spencer told Peace. "I don't trust that polecat for a minute and I want to know where he's headed. It's too late to try any trailing tonight, so we'll see if your men can pick up any information. Then we'll slip out before dawn — so you won't have to argue with any nosey pickets."

The sergeant grinned. "No arguments," he said loftily. "My orders was to keep ye in sight. Nobuddy said we couldn't go outa camp."

The evening was not what Spencer had earlier contemplated. He had been looking forward to spending some time with Ruth. Instead, getting ready for the morning's scout occupied his full attention. Weapons and clothing had to be prepared and Sergeant Peace showed his understanding of the situation by bringing in a supply of the jerked beef which had been frozen into slabs for winter use.

The only information they could procure was that Curt Donnel had left the camp with the men who were going to risk the trip east. Donnel was mounted and well equipped. The others were afoot.

Finally, in spite of the care they had to take in order that an observer might not suspect their intention, everything was in readiness. The two horses Spencer and Ruth had used on the trip to Fort Bridger were picketed nearby and the program was outlined to Major Pierce.

"You'll not be hindered, I think," the major said calmly. "Marcy was supposed to leave the Henry's Fork camp today. That means any other men detailed to watch you will have been relieved. Good luck."

"If everything is right I'll be back in two days," Spencer told him. "If there's signs of something wrong, Peace will tell you about it."

They let it go at that, understanding each other without the need for lengthy explanation.

To Ruth, Spencer was a little more explicit. "I've got a nasty hunch that Donnel is up to something," he said soberly. "When they were looking for men to guide Marcy's outfit, he kept quiet about his knowledge of the country, but he's been around here plenty. He certainly can guess that Marcy knows my story — and Marcy is headed for the country where this man Garcia hangs out."

"You think he might try to do something to Captain Marcy?"

"It's possible. Marcy's death would put him in the clear for a while."

"But will he know that?"

"It wouldn't take much guessing for him to think so — and he'd be right, I imagine. One way or another,

I've got to make sure that he isn't up to some more of his dirty work. This army can't afford to lose Marcy."

She smiled quietly. "I thought you had gotten to the point of not caring about the army."

"I thought so too. Maybe I'm only worried about Marcy."

"No. I think it's a little of both. Marcy's your friend but you still have a sense of duty. Years of bitterness haven't killed it — and I'm glad."

"I'm a little afraid of you," he told her, his smile a little crooked. "You see straight through a fellow — and at rather short notice. Maybe it wouldn't be safe for me to be around you all winter."

"Is that a hint that you're regretting what you said last night?"

"Not for a minute. I'll be back. Maybe in a couple of days. Maybe later. But I'll be back."

"And I'll be waiting. Remember that always."

A bit of sleet in the bitter predawn blackness when Spencer and Sergeant Peace slipped away from the camp warned Spencer that no time was to be lost. He would have to depend on sign to learn what he wanted to know and a snowfall could ruin everything.

They evaded the pickets without trouble, striking off across the ridge beyond the cliffs. "Black's Fork flows east and joins Ham's Fork in a few miles," Spencer explained. "We'll make a short cut for two reasons. It ought to keep us clear of Mormon scouts and it'll tell us something in a hurry. If Donnel is going east with his men he'll ride back over the trail the way the army marched. If he's heading for Taos he'll leave his men to follow the old trail while he cuts down Black's Fork to reach the Green. It'll save him miles and trouble."

When daylight broke they were moving downgrade toward the lower bend of Black's Fork. They had encountered no sign that any Mormons had been riding in this area. It seemed likely that their outposts would be closer to Fort Bridger and Echo Canyon.

The sleet had subsided but the cold was still bitter when they reached the partly frozen stream. Spencer halted at once, studying the single line of tracks which marked the passage of a rider.

"Army-shod mule," he grunted. "That the way you make it?"

"Nothin' else," Peace agreed. "Ye reckon it was Donnel?"

"Hard to tell much about the age of tracks in this kind of weather, but I'm guessing it was. The Mormons don't ride mules."

He worked along the trail with care, studying the particles of sleet which had lodged in the tiny depressions. Much of the track on the hard frozen ground was completely unreadable, but in places the rider had ventured rather close to the edge of the swift-flowing stream, and there the story could be worked out.

"Can you find your way back over the ridge?" Spencer asked shortly.

"I reckon."

"Good. Let me have that jerky and your spare rifle ammunition. Tell Major Pierce — and Miss Corliss."

The sergeant grinned as he handed over the articles requested. "Me, I'd tell her myself," he declared. "It ain't sensible fer a man to go ramblin' around the winter mountains with a gal like that in camp."

"I'm not very sensible," Spencer retorted. "Now get on your way before somebody comes along to adopt you into the Saints. I've got to hustle it up before snow flies. Watch yourself on the way back."

"Listen to the man!" Peace jeered. "Tellin' me to be keerful! Git goin' now before I remember I'm supposed to keep an eye on ye."

They shook hands and then Spencer headed his bronc down Black's Fork, studying the faint sign and trying to estimate the amount of distance between himself and the man he was trailing. He did not look back to see what Sergeant Peace was doing.

He halted only once during the day, picking a spot where the stream widened a little to provide some meadow forage for the horse. The grazing wasn't good, but it was better than anything he had seen. Although he chafed at the delay he took time to let the animal have his fill. Keeping a horse under him on this trip was going to be a problem.

He calculated that he was within a mile or so of Green River when he made camp for the night, choosing his spot again because of the forage. The threat of snow still hung in the air but it seemed useless to plunge ahead.

He was on the move again at an early hour, leading the horse through the darkness both for the sake of caution and to keep the animal as fresh as possible.

There might be Mormon scouting parties along the Green and he didn't want to be trapped by them.

Daylight found him at the confluence of Black's Fork and Green River. A definite spit of snow prompted him to get on with his sign-reading as quickly as possible. The mule tracks were still clear and he saw that his quarry had paused here just long enough to search the ground. Donnel, and he did not doubt the identity of the unseen mule rider, had searched for sign and found none. Marcy's party had not come this way, as they would certainly have done if they were intending to strike eastward before moving south. Apparently they had worked southeast from Henry's Fork to strike the Green at some more southerly spot. Donnel must have figured it that way, for he had gone on downstream.

Three miles farther on, Spencer found the camp where Donnel had spent the night. That meant an interval of perhaps five miles between them. Maybe less if Donnel had not started so early in the morning.

An hour before dusk he found the other sign he had been expecting. A large party of mounted men, most of them on mules, had come out of the hills to swing south along the Green. Donnel's tracks blended with the others, but Spencer knew that the single rider must be a full day behind Marcy's party.

Snow fell heavily that night, but he did not mind it too much. The temperature rose with the snowfall until probably it was a shade above the zero mark. At least it did not feel so bitter and Spencer lost that vague, haunting dread which had been nagging at him. The danger of frostbite was not so great now. At zero a man could take care of himself. Below that he was always in danger — and so was his horse.

Again he camped with daylight to spare, this time selecting a stand of pine where the snow had not filtered through the heavy branches. The spot didn't offer much forage for the already starving horse, but it was as good as any other place. Finding graze for a horse under four inches of new snow was a constant problem, particularly in this stretch of mountains. But Spencer did not allow himself to get sentimental about it, even though he had been riding this horse since leaving Kansas. It was almost a dead cinch that the trip would kill the animal. All he could do was to get the most out of him while he managed to survive.

At dawn he moved on under lowering skies which threatened a new snowfall. The thought made him push matters a little more than he had been doing. He wanted to study this trail quite a bit before closing in on Captain Marcy's company, but he didn't want to get so far behind them that a heavy snowfall might cut off all sign.

Within the first hour of riding he found two camps, the first one Donnel's. Again he estimated the interval between himself and his old enemy, realizing that a day of travel had cut it down considerably. Curt's mule was not doing as well as the horse. Since Donnel had camped directly along the river where rocky banks left no forage at all, it seemed certain that his pace would continue to slow. A man with Donnel's wilderness experience wouldn't risk his mount any more than circumstances required.

The other camp was not more than a half mile beyond Donnel's. Its sign was plain but unreadable for it was covered with yesterday's snow. Spencer could only guess at the time Marcy had left Henry's Fork, but it seemed likely that the party was setting a rather fast pace. At least they had reached the Green a full day ahead of Donnel. Even granting that they had part of a day's start from a more southerly camp, there was still the matter of travel conditions. Marcy had been forced to cut across country through Mormon pickets while Donnel had used a relatively open trail along streams. So far Marcy and his men were doing better than all right.

The afternoon brought more snow, but it was not heavy and Spencer elected to hold back, at times walking his horse and always letting the animal set his own pace. For the present he had certain advantages. He had other people breaking trail for him and he knew about Donnel without the other man having knowledge of a trailer. Unless weather conditions intervened, he decided to keep it that way until he could determine what was happening.

For three consecutive days it snowed a little every afternoon. There was never enough of it to cause any great trouble, but the succession of snow layers permitted rather accurate sign reading. At the end of the third day Spencer knew that he was less than an hour's travel behind Donnel, perhaps three hours behind Marcy's party. The larger group was beginning to lag now, apparently having to fit the pace to the slower members of the company. That was the trouble with such a unit in the wilderness. One man or a pair of them could out-travel a larger outfit any time.

Spencer was a little puzzled about the size of Marcy's detachment. He knew that there were some sixty horses and mules ahead, but he could only guess as to the number carrying riders. Camp sites were too confused for more than a hasty guess, but he estimated that perhaps half of the sixty animals were carrying packs or were replacement mounts. Since the available beasts on Henry's Fork were known to be few, there was a strong possibility that the proportion was even smaller.

Twice after that Spencer camped within sight of a fire which he knew would be Curt Donnel's. By this time he was avoiding fire for himself. The jerky wasn't worth cooking and it seemed like a bigger meal if he had to chew on it a little longer.

In another day or so, he realized, he would have to alter his program. He had been holding back to estimate what Donnel might be planning, but very quickly now he would have to do one thing or another: drop back far enough to do some hunting or push on to join the main force. For the present Donnel seemed to be playing a game just like his own. He was hanging close on the rear of Marcy's party but he certainly was not trying to overtake them.

It bothered Spencer to see that the guides ahead were sticking to the valley of the Green. By not cutting southeast so as to cross the Colorado above the junction, they were adding unnecessary distance to the journey. Playing it safe, he thought. Nobody knew the mountains well enough to take chances on the unmarked country.

Several times he almost made up his mind to ride ahead and offer his services, but each time he thought better of it.

He knew that the problem of food supply would soon take the decision out of his hands, but he intended to wait as long as possible. The wait proved to be shorter than he had anticipated. Just as he was preparing to make camp in a convenient stand of aspens, he caught the sound of a gunshot from the trail ahead. It was followed swiftly by a second one and then silence.

For an instant he considered the possibility that Donnel might have resorted to hunting. Then he knew better. Curt was hanging so close upon the flanks of the Marcy party — and had been doing that for so long — that it seemed obvious he intended to keep himself unknown to them. Under the circumstances he would not be advertising himself with gunfire.

Spencer sent his weary horse plunging ahead through the crusted snow, ignoring the rifle in its saddle scabbard but bringing out one of the Colts to check its loads and caps. Handling a revolver while wearing buffalo mittens was clumsy work, but he managed to satisfy himself that the weapon was in working order. Then he thrust it into the front of his jacket, loosening the right-hand mitten so as to be ready for instant action. If Donnel had ambushed Marcy with any intentions of beating a hasty retreat, Spencer intended to have something to say about it.

Suddenly he checked his pace. His guesses had been all wrong. A new factor had entered the deal. Three riders on unshod ponies had come out of the woodland to follow the well-marked trail of mules and horses.

"Utes!" he exclaimed half aloud. "Hunting party. I wonder if Donnel saw them first?"

CHAPTER SIXTEEN

Spencer calculated with care. Those shots had come downwind to him through a shallow gulch, probably from a distance of something over a half mile. Already he had ridden more than half of that distance, so it behooved him to be cautious. The Indians might be lying in wait — or he could run into an ambush bullet from Curt Donnel.

Then he glimpsed a thin trickle of smoke rising from a thicket of spruce. Evidently Donnel had been making camp when the Utes appeared. Spencer swung his mount aside into a little thicker cover, keeping his right hand inside the coat so that the icy revolver would not be too numbing to bare flesh. The smoke was maybe four hundred yards ahead; somewhere in the same region were enemies.

He had closed the interval to less than two hundred yards when another rifle shot crashed on the frigid air. This time he was in a position to witness its effect. An almost-naked Indian drove a shaggy pony hard out of the spruces, disappearing promptly down a slope where larger trees hid him almost immediately.

"Dam' Digger Injuns!" Spencer growled in his throat. "Bare hide to zero weather and don't seem to mind it a bit." The words were little more than a cover for his inner thoughts. He was considering what he knew about Utes. They were thieves and scavengers rather than warriors. Maybe Donnel had beaten them off. If so, where were the other two?

He could guess at the answer but he did not take unnecessary risks. Curt Donnel and two dead Indians ahead would mean a greater danger than a dead Donnel and two hostile savages.

Dusk was making visibility poor when he picketed his bronc and cautiously moved forward on foot.

Once he froze in his tracks, the revolver out and ready, but he caught a glimpse of a riderless pony blundering among the firs. That seemed to fit. Only one Indian had retreated. Donnel must have defended himself rather well.

He could see the glow of a tiny twig fire when he worked around the next clump of firs. No one stirred near the fire, but a dark object made a blur on the ground not twenty feet ahead. He moved up cautiously and discovered the dead body of a Ute. The Indian had been killed instantly by a slug through the chest. Probably the former owner of that loose pony, he decided. That left Donnel and another Indian still to be accounted for.

He was racing the darkness now, but he did not let it stampede him into any rash moves. Circling slightly toward the more-open country, he spotted a flicker of movement and realized that he was watching an Indian crawling painfully through the snowy bushes. The savage was armed only with bow and arrow, but he was holding himself ready. Almost at the same instant Spencer could see the brief movement which indicated Donnel's position. Curt and the Ute were only a few feet away from each other with little concealment for either. Why didn't Donnel fire?

He waited until the Ute inched forward another twenty feet toward the thicket where Donnel was hiding. Every second he expected to hear the slam of a rifle, but the woodland remained silent except for the whisper of the wind in the conifers. Even when the Indian exposed himself to cross from one bush to another there was no attempt to stop him. Now Spencer could see that the Ute had been shot badly, the left leg broken at the thigh. He was trailing blood as he crawled and must have known that he could not expect to survive such a wound in this weather. Still he dragged himself forward, clearly determined to kill the white man who had crippled him.

At first Spencer had figured to wait for Donnel to kill the injured savage, then to close in while Curt was reloading. Now he knew that he would have to change his program. Donnel must be wounded also — and badly. Otherwise that miserable Ute wouldn't have lived so long.

He crept forward a few feet, trying to keep cover between himself and both danger spots. Presently he could see a foot sticking out from behind a fair-sized spruce. Its toe was pointed skyward.

Almost as he saw it he realized that the Indian was gathering himself for a final effort, hauling himself to a twisted sitting position so that he could draw his bow.

The hunting arrow was already notched when Spencer drew fine with the Colt and blasted two quick shots. Then he ducked to one side, getting clear of the powder smoke which hung like a wraith on cold air.

Nothing happened. The Ute was motionless now, sprawled out in the snow. Beyond the fir tree the boot toe still pointed up. Spencer decided to risk a trap. With night coming down he had little choice.

Crouching low, he sprang forward with gun in hand. It was not needed. Curt Donnel was lying flat on his back, his rifle at his side and the shaft of an arrow sticking out of his chest. He was breathing but there was blood at his mouth and down the side of his beard. Spencer felt under him and discovered that the arrow had not gone through. That was bad. A shaft could be cut and pulled through sometimes. When the barbarous point was lodged inside the body it required expert surgery to remove it without killing the patient.

A new sound came to him then and he took cover. Not far away, a foot had broken snow crust. Perhaps the third Ute had recovered from his scare and was coming back. He remained motionless for perhaps three minutes, tracing the sound of stealthy movement as it approached. Then he drew a breath of relief as a muffled figure was briefly outlined against a patch of still-light sky.

"You're gettin' clumsy, Cal," he called. "Any deaf squaw would have caught you foul on this one."

"How's that?" Trent's voice came, astonishment and relief blending in the tones. "That you, Spencer?"

"Over here. Looks like we got a problem. Donnel's goin' to die."

Cal Trent didn't ask any questions. If he had expected to find Donnel and Spencer out here in the snow, he would have been no more casual. "That ain't no problem," he grunted. "Kinda what yuh might call a public improvement."

"Give me a hand with him. I want to see if we can get a word or two out of him."

Trent waited only long enough to whistle a single shrill note, then he came through the trees to where Spencer still knelt beside Curt Donnel. "Injuns," he said softly, staring at the arrow. "I kinda figgered it was a family fight."

"I wanted him alive," Spencer said.

"So I figgered after what the cap'n told me. It kinda had me puzzled." He chuckled dryly as he added, "Not that I calc'lated to find either of ye back here when we heard the shootin'. Any more o' the red pests around?"

"I don't think so. I found the trail of three of them and I saw one high-tailin' it for home. Donnel killed one and wounded another. That was the buck I just finished."

Three of Marcy's mounted infantrymen pounded clumsily into view, their bulky, swaddled figures looming out of proportion to the skinny mules they were riding.

"Try to move him on to your camp as fast as you can," Spencer told Cal. "If he talks listen. I'm going back to find my horse. And don't let your men get itchy with their trigger fingers. I'll be back pronto and I've got a sharp prejudice against being mistaken for a Ute."

It took a little time to find the bronc in the gloom and when he returned to the scene of the skirmish it was fully dark. Trent and the infantrymen had not left. They had located Donnel's mule, but they were not having much luck in getting the unconscious man to stay in the saddle.

"He keeps slidin' off," Trent complained. "And the dang longear's too weak to carry another man."

"You'll kill him the way you're doing," Spencer snapped. "Get a rider around on that other side to hold him. Then a couple of you prop him up while I range in on this side. If we keep the horses close we'll get him in."

"Horses, hell!" a soldier growled. "Yuh can't make these mules behave nohow!"

They tried to carry out the instructions, however, and the little group moved off, though Spencer soon found that he had most of the work to do. It was a ticklish business but somehow he managed it, covering the scant mile tediously but without losing his man. He could only hope that the rough handling had not been fatal. More than anything else at that moment, he wanted to hear Curt Donnel talk. A dying man might be ready to make a decent gesture.

Willing hands came to assist without asking and Donnel was soon stretched out beside a brush fire. Captain Marcy asked no questions. He simply nodded when Spencer said, "He's dying," and went across to a pile of packs. When he returned he held a flask which he tilted gently to Donnel's lips. More blood was coming now, but the wounded man was swallowing, so there seemed to be a possibility that the stimulant might bring him around.

There was a long interval in which no one spoke. The men grouped around the fire were not even moving as they watched the strange tableau which they could not understand. Only in the outer portions of the camp were voices clear as noncoms sent out more guards, obviously thinking that the camp was in danger of an Indian attack.

Suddenly Donnel swallowed hard and a groan came through, a horrible bubbling sort of groan that brought extra shivers to the watchers. Then the black eyes opened, staring almost sightlessly at the dim forms silhouetted in the firelight. "Dam' Utes!" he whispered. "I —"

A gush of blood shut off the whisper and a convulsive shudder went over him. The eyes remained open but they were sightless now. Curt Donnel was dead.

Marcy fumbled for a wrist, holding it for a minute or two before straightening up. "That's all," he said shortly. "Now tell me what this is all about."

Spencer told him in some detail. The early parts of the story Marcy had to pry out of him by some close questioning, but eventually they understood each other quite well.

"So he has been hanging on our rear for almost two weeks, eh?" Marcy muttered. "That sure makes it look like he was up to no good. Maybe I don't feel so sorry for him now as I did when I was watching him die."

Spencer did not reply. He had known no feeling of compunction at all and he did not propose to be hypocritical about it. Donnel deserved his fate — but it was inconvenient to have it happen just now. More than likely it marked the end of a nine-year quest.

There was a general conference that night, only the men on picket duty remaining away. Almost all discipline had been dropped and it was clear that Marcy had taken his men into a sort of partnership. They had to realize that each man's life depended upon cooperation with the others and it seemed better to handle it informally.

Spencer disposed of the Indian threat at once, assuring them that there was very little chance of attack. The three Utes had been a hunting party who had tried to pick off a man they probably thought was a straggler from the main force.

"No reason to relax vigilance, of course," Spencer warned, "but the big problem is to get across country faster. You've been swinging too far to the west. You should have left the Green a couple of days ago. The Colorado crossing will be easier farther up and the distance will be quite a few miles less."

"You're the guide now," Marcy told him. "We'll follow you."

"We hope," Spencer countered. "The mules I saw don't look like they'd follow anybody very far."

"How much farther will it be?"

"Four hundred miles, at a guess. Mostly harder travel than what you've seen so far. Do your men have snowshoes?"

"No."

"Then we'll make some. Every camp we'll work on it. If the mules last until we're all outfitted, we'll be able to push on without mounts when we have to. If we get some heavy snow, we may have to abandon the animals anyway."

They buried Curt Donnel that night, piling rocks over the body to protect it from coyotes or prowling Indians. Marcy searched the pockets first, but Donnel had been too clever a crook to carry anything incriminating.

It came as a surprise to Spencer that his own bitter disappointment should subside so quickly. Donnel's death had been a blow to his hopes, but at the same time he was relieved of the tension under which he had been working. No longer was he alone on the trail, trying to time every movement without regard to his own convenience. Tonight he could sleep in a guarded camp and know that there would be fire for some sort of hot food in the morning. Probably it would be roasted mule meat, but it would be better than no breakfast at all. The prospect seemed almost luxurious.

Dawn found him more rested than he had been since leaving the Black's Fork camp. He made a brief scout around the bivouac while the pack mules were being loaded, well content to find no sign of Indians. After that he stood aside to watch the column move out along the river, checking his own estimate of the numbers. There were thirty-five enlisted men, all show of rank completely hidden under the huge buffalo coats with which they were provided. They were dirty, bearded and grim but there was a touch of humor in much of the grimness and he decided that they were a good outfit for a journey like this. With Marcy to command, Cal Trent to scout the flanks, and himself as guide, they would get through. He would have bet on it.

Two hours later he was not so sure. The overcast which had blotted out the brief sunrise had been closing down on the higher peaks until it seemed almost smothering. Now it let loose a heavy fall of huge snowflakes, the kind that cover men and animals too rapidly to be brushed off.

By noon they were working through a narrow pass in a blinding blizzard, leaving Green River behind them. It seemed like a bad time to exchange easily distinguishable landmarks for the wilderness of broken rock which stretched away to the east, and Spencer halted the column before making the turn. "It's not the way I'd cross to the Colorado," he told Marcy, "but it's passable. I think it's better than going farther out of our way."

"You're the guide," Marcy said. "Lead the way."

There seemed to be no grumbling among the men even though they must have viewed the prospect with some misgivings. That was a compliment to Captain Marcy, Spencer thought. Men who had volunteered for this assignment were willing to trust him all the way. There was something fine about being a leader like Marcy, something to restore confidence in human nature, almost enough to restore confidence in the army.

He put the thought aside hastily, just as he had refused on several occasions to let himself think of Ruth Corliss. For the present he had to discard all forms of emotion or sentiment. The lives of thirty-seven men depended upon his judgment and decisions. Nothing must interfere.

He kept that resolution for three full days, partly because conditions would not let him forget it. The snow fell constantly, the rising wind bringing a drop in temperature which threatened men and animals with frostbite. This was the real blizzard he had been dreading, the angry outpouring of winter's bile which would spell disaster to everyone. Everyone was walking now, partly to save the staggering animals and partly because activity was the only thing that would keep them from freezing. By the end of the second day men were fighting panic just as the animals were fighting exhaustion and the snow banks. There would be no respite for either. Danger and cold would go hand in hand.

In midafternoon of the third day of the blizzard, Spencer found the valley he had been almost afraid to hope was there. Approaching from this angle he had not been too certain of finding it, but the column struck it on schedule. Towering cliffs on the north and west offered the best possible protection against the wintry winds, while a gentle slope to the south offered hope that the exhausted animals could find some sort of forage under the snow. Along the little creek which flowed beneath the rimrock there was even a trace of green where the winds had kept the snow moving. It was the most sheltered spot they had seen in days and Marcy gave orders to prepare for a rest until the worst of the blizzard should subside. Better to lose a little time than to push forward with animals dying along the trail.

CHAPTER SEVENTEEN

For the men the valley camp was no rest period. Part of the force was kept busy scraping snow so that horses and mules might nibble at the frozen grasses beneath. Another half dozen were employed at the continuing business of making snowshoes. Everyone had a turn at gathering firewood.

Spencer and Trent scouted the valley even before the blizzard subsided, bringing in two deer and some small game along with the information that no Indian villages were in the vicinity. For the moment the only enemy was old General Winter, a tough and merciless antagonist who seemed to need no allies.

Clearing skies sent them forward through hip-deep snow on the twenty-third of December, most of the frostbite victims a little improved by the rest and comparative shelter. Matters were not so favorable with the stock. There had been forage enough in the valley to keep them alive but it had been too sparse to bring back any of the strength they had lost. Loads had to be divided among all of the remaining beasts, leaving none to carry riders. Not that anyone thought of riding. The snow was too deep and the cold too intense. Men walked to keep from freezing, at the same time knowing that they had no choice in the matter. The life of every horse and mule in the column was something to be preserved by every means possible.

Christmas marked the beginning of the expected die-off. Four mules and a horse had to be killed during the day's freezing march. Each was butchered promptly, the stringy flesh welcome enough as supplies began to run dangerously low.

During the ensuing week they lost thirty-odd head of stock, even though a new snowfall kept them idle for a full day. Rest could do little for animals without forage. The first of January found them along the Gunnison with twenty mules and Spencer's saddle horse still alive. Men were carrying the extra ammunition and weapons now, better able to handle the loads than were the tottering beasts. The extra food supply was exhausted, and for two days the only rations had been horse and mule meat. They no longer waited for stock to collapse, they simply shot the weakest animals when it was time for a meal.

Then the coldest weather of the journey struck. No one had been foolish enough to burden himself with even so small a useless item as a thermometer, so they could only guess at the actual temperature. Spencer estimated that it went to twenty-five below zero. Most of the soldiers insisted that it was much lower. At any rate, it meant an increased danger of frostbite and a new threat to the animals. Now the mules were freezing to death instead of dropping from exhaustion and starvation.

A solid week of it killed off the remaining animals. Men were plowing ahead on their snowshoes now, doggedly trying to make progress and avoid freezing, each carrying his own share of the frozen meat which had been cut from the dead animals. With proper care their emergency rations would last an additional week. Within that period they would have to find extra food or face the same starvation that had marked the end of the stock.

Trent and Spencer were ranging far ahead of the column each day, hoping to sight game, but the cold seemed to have driven every creature to cover. They killed only one small doe in a week of this sort of hunting — and such a supply of venison did not go far with thirty-seven men.

Still the little column floundered on through the snow, men with frostbitten feet half-carried by comrades who were in little better condition. They were gaunt and haggard, their beards crusted with ice that had not broken loose for days. At night they huddled together for such warmth as a nearby body could provide. In the morning they had to break themselves apart, knock the breath-frost from their turned-up collars, and plunge on once more.

No one talked very much, no man wanting to let that icy air get into his mouth. It was bad enough to take a deep breath when the cold of it made lungs ache. Still they were doggedly grim, knowing that there could be no respite, no surrender. Every man had to keep going; to do otherwise meant death. Under Marcy's persistent prodding they shambled onward, crossing mountains and streams, forests and badlands. No one but Spencer and Trent seemed to be conscious of the terrain. For the men of the Fifth Infantry it was just one snow-covered mile after another.

The carefully rationed mule meat gave out on the fifteenth of January and for thirty-six hours no one tasted food. The cold snap eased, however, and some of Spencer's diligence was rewarded on the second day of the fast. Less than a half mile ahead of the column he knocked over a large buck. Only an hour later Trent killed an even larger one.

That night the little company camped in the shelter of a good stand of pine, warming themselves around well-stoked fires and relaxing with well-filled bellies. Even the frostbite sufferers seemed to get some relief, and for the first time in a fortnight men made feeble jokes.

Spencer carefully refrained from saying anything that would remind them of the hard days which lay ahead. He had been increasingly worried over the silence that lay over every camp, recalling the instances he had seen of men going winter-crazy. Some people simply could not stand the constant danger, vigilance and hardship. Maybe this break in the tension would keep away the dread specter of panic. Men with hope would keep trying instead of letting themselves go to pieces.

They made astonishingly good progress for the next two days, but then the weather seemed to gather itself for a final deadly assault. A howling northerly blizzard swept out of the arctic wastes, icing the snow crust with a cutting sleet storm which blinded any man who tried to see where he was going. Travel became impossible and game was not to be found.

They went into camp when they could do nothing else, huddling together miserably with no food and almost no fuel. For two days they remained at that spot, getting almost no rest because they had to keep moving to avoid freezing. After the bitter second night it was no great surprise to anyone when a trooper named Collins failed to roll out in the morning.

"Poor devil," Marcy said softly. "For two weeks he has been marching on frozen feet. A man with that much nerve deserved to win through."

No one else seemed disposed to comment. The captain's words had been requiem enough. Maybe Collins was the lucky one. He would not have to face another hundred miles of this torture.

They left Collins deep in a snowbank when an additional fall of snow covered the ice crust sufficiently for travel to be possible. The cold had relaxed a little with the new snow and Spencer moved on ahead, promising them that game would be moving soon. It wasn't much of a promise, he knew, but he was trying to keep up those thin hopes.

That night he felt easier than he had been since leaving Black's Fork. Not only had they killed enough game so that every man had a decent ration, but the country was sloping off into the sort of terrain he knew as New Mexico. Landmarks were hard to distinguish, but he had a feeling that the end was almost in sight.

Just past noon on the following day his premonition proved accurate. They crossed a low ridge and saw a group of buildings below them. One of the buildings was evidently a ranch house. Smoke was coming out of a chimney and men were moving about near a stable. Farther across the valley cattle were trampling the snow, evidently feeding on stored hay.

Spencer pointed ahead as the first soldiers came up to him. "I hope that rancher isn't planning to build up a herd with that stock," he remarked, his grin cracking the icy crust on his beard. "He'll put in a big bill to the government for what you boys are going to eat."

A hoarse cheer went back along the line. For almost two months the volunteers of the Fifth had been fighting a desperate battle with winter. Now victory was in sight.

They were still a ragged-looking lot when they trudged into Taos on the afternoon of the twenty-second, but none of them cared about that. A good rest on clean hay and plenty of well-cooked food had done wonders for them. Already they had ceased to talk about their own troubles and were discussing the new problem of getting beef cattle back to the army.

Spencer remained in Taos just long enough to learn what Marcy's plans would be. The army post commander at Taos was eagerly cooperative, but it quickly became apparent that it would take time to round up the necessary number of cattle. Herders would also have to be employed and Marcy's men would require mounts. Even if the weather should permit cattle drives, there seemed to be little likelihood of the return trip starting in less than two months. Couriers would be sent out to all points, requesting assistance, and Spencer easily secured the duty of carrying a message to Santa Fe.

He reached that city on the last day of January, delivering his dispatches and spending an hour with the commandant. In exchange for his story of the winter he received some of the information he wanted. A man named Garcia was indeed a freighter in Santa Fe. He was also a cattle dealer, a gambler and many other things which no one could prove. Spencer gathered that Señor Garcia was a genial sort of scoundrel. Even the post commander grinned when he spoke of some of the crooked deals the man had been suspected of making.

Maybe that was good, Spencer thought. Garcia had nothing to fear. His part in the war had been formally pardoned. Perhaps the man would be willing to talk.

That cheerful thought perished slowly. For a week he prowled the streets of Santa Fe, visiting cantinas and searching for some clue to the whereabouts of the man he wanted. It was no problem to find men who knew Garcia. Everyone knew something about him — and most of the knowledge was the kind that made men grin or wink to recall. Garcia was a character. The difficulty was that no one knew of his present whereabouts.

By the end of February Spencer was as disgusted as he had been during those long weeks of trailing Curt Donnel. Now it was not a matter of personal danger but of exasperation. Everything he learned made him feel that Garcia might be persuaded to talk — but he couldn't find Garcia. Once he rode as far east as Tucumcari and on another occasion to Albuquerque, both times on false scents. Garcia had been there but was not on hand for Spencer.

In both places Spencer added to his store of knowledge about the man. He was now certain that Garcia was indeed the guerrilla leader of the late war. Everything pointed to the man as being the one person who could — and perhaps would — clear Spencer's name.

On the second of March, Spencer got his first good lead. He had stopped in at the military post to learn what he could about preparations for Marcy's cattle drive and was surprised to hear that the War Department was now taking valiant steps to relieve the army at Fort Bridger. More men were going out from Kansas as soon as the trails were passable and Marcy was to take reinforcements from Taos. Already men were being selected for the duty from posts in the area. At the same time a huge cattle herd was being collected on the upper Canadian — and one of the dealers providing the beef was Señor Garcia.

That night Spencer started for Taos, riding until he was weary and then camping along the trail. Time was running out and he didn't propose to lose his man by wasting time in Santa Fe.

Two nights later he rode his jaded horse into Taos and went at once to the military post. The town seemed quiet and there were no soldiers in the narrow old streets. He didn't think Marcy's expedition could possibly have started yet, but still he didn't like the look of it. Was this to be another of those close misses?

The explanation was simple but exasperating. Marcy had moved his headquarters to Rayados, where the beef herds were concentrating. The extra troop units were with him at that point, ready for the march northward. Spencer gave up. He proposed to get a decent night's rest no matter what happened next. A man could stand just so much of chasing a will-o'-the-wisp like Garcia.

After that he took it easy, riding into the Rayados camp as though he did not have a care in the world. He even passed a couple of cattle outfits without asking questions. Garcia wouldn't be with his beef anyway; he would be closeted with some supply officer, trying to make a fast deal.

In spite of his self-imposed attitude of wry resignation, he could not help but be impressed by what he saw. Huge temporary corrals held hundreds of horses and mules. Beef herds were held in the valleys by *vaqueros* aided by mounted troopers. The tents of some four hundred soldiers had been pitched along the bank of the river. Clearly the government was preparing to strike the Mormons with sufficient force to end the trouble without further delay.

He found Marcy's headquarters, but finding Marcy was like finding Garcia. The captain was evidently trying to put his force together as swiftly and as efficiently as possible and attending to most details in person. Every time Spencer asked a question he was directed to some spot which Marcy had just left. After an hour, he turned his mount and went back to the captain's tent.

"I'm tired of hunting people," he grumbled to himself. "I think I'll just sit down and wait for somebody to find me."

Ten minutes later Captain Marcy and an immaculately dressed Mexican rode up and dismounted. "Glad to see you back, Spencer," Marcy greeted, his smile a trifle crooked. "We'll be needing you around here. And let me introduce you to one of the men who is supplying us with beef cattle. Dan Spencer, Señor Jose Garcia."

Spencer forgot his manners. All he said was, "Well, I'll be damned!"

Both Marcy and Garcia laughed, but it was the Mexican who spoke first. "I think I understand your feeling," he said, only the faintest accent discernible in his careful tones. "The good captain and I have discussed your unhappy difficulties at some length. My apologies for the trouble I have caused you."

"I tried to reach you," Marcy explained, "but apparently you did not get my message. Señor Garcia was quite willing to make a formal statement and it is now on its way to Washington."

"The captain does me too much credit," Garcia suggested. "A man like myself does not brag of his misdeeds. We made — shall we say — a deal."

Marcy smiled. "Some of the cattle Señor Garcia delivered to me were a bit questionable. Some of the brands were slightly irregular, if you understand what I mean. I spoke to him about it and he agreed to see that they were restored to their proper owners — and to sign the statement we mentioned. In return I agreed to accept the rest of his herd without prejudice — and without making any report on the 'strays' that were with his beef."

"Carelessness on the part of my *vaqueros,"* Garcia added with a shrug.

These two were obviously enjoying their facetious humor and Spencer saw no reason why he should not join in. "I hope you gentlemen will not publish this," he said solemnly. "It will be a terrible blow to the moral writers who dream up tales about virtue and diligence being rewarded in the end. I spend nine years trying to get a line on Curt Donnel. So a miserable Ute kills him. Then I spend six weeks hunting a certain Jose Garcia and all I do is listen to entertaining tales about his exploits. Next I spend two hours hunting for Captain Marcy. After that I get disgusted and sit down. Immediately two fairy godmothers in disguise come along and fix up all my troubles without me having to do another thing. This will completely ruin the virtue and diligence business if word ever gets out."

Marcy laughed but the Mexican nodded in solemn agreement. "It will be our secret," he said firmly. "And now, Captain, shall we conclude our business? Not being virtuous, I must double my diligence and ride back to Santa Fe where other business awaits."

"You'll excuse us, Spencer?" Marcy asked courteously. "Señor Garcia and I will be finished in but a moment. Then I'll want to see you."

Spencer nodded. In spite of his quizzical speech he was still feeling a little numb.

CHAPTER EIGHTEEN

Preparations for the drive were rushed to completion during the next ten days. For Dan Spencer the time dragged wearily. It was gratifying to know that Marcy had written a lengthy report in which Spencer was given full credit for the successful march to Taos, even more pleasant to know that Garcia's statement had gone forward with that report, but both matters seemed insignificant now that they were affairs of the past. The big consideration now was to reach that winter-bound army on Black's Fork.

Spencer had wanted to act as messenger for Captain Marcy when a report was sent ahead to Colonel Johnston, but Marcy objected. "We'll need you later," he said quietly. "No one in camp seems to know the country north of the Arkansas. I'm depending on you to see us through."

Spencer could not argue. He owed much to Marcy's good will and he could not let impatience carry him away. So Cal Trent went north with the message and Spencer remained to fret over his own inactivity. With no particular duties to occupy his mind, he found himself worrying over many matters which had not even crossed his mind since December. Had rations held out over the winter? Had discipline been maintained in the camp or had the unruly teamsters broken out into riot? Had sickness of any sort swept the camp?

It was easy to imagine all sorts of things having happened to Ruth, and he found himself imagining all of them. His own new status was almost forgotten. What the War Department would do about his case no longer mattered; all he wanted was to find Ruth and get her back to civilization.

It was a relief when he was called into conference with Captain Marcy and several other officers. They wanted his advice and he gave it promptly, aware that they were listening with a show of respect. He wondered about it almost without real interest. Did they know his story or were they simply listening to a scout who had proved his mettle?

On the fourteenth of March the beef herds were set in motion to the northwest with competent herders handling them. There were three separate herds, each ramroded by a trail boss who knew the country well. They were to move their stock away from the Canadian so as to cross the Purgatoire, the Huerfano and the Arkansas well to the west of Bent's Fort, thus avoiding any deep-water crossings. For the first two hundred miles the beef herds would pick the trail but after the Arkansas crossing Spencer would take charge and act as guide. For the present he was to stay ahead of the herds with Marcy's veterans, serving principally as a scouting party.

Spring had come early and the valleys were drying out quickly enough to make travel reasonably easy. On the second day of the movement Spencer used much of the time for instructing his mounted infantrymen in the tricks of scouting. The bitter march southward had taught them a lot and they were willing to learn from the man who had brought them through. There were no McGees or Trents among them, but they were learning fast and Spencer had no fears about the advance guard doing its duty well.

Partly to let them have the feel of responsibility, he selected the following day to ride back along the column. The sight brought a reaction that surprised him. For years he had been viewing military units and army posts with a jaundiced eye. Now he studied the marching arrangements with satisfaction and something that was almost like pride. His own dubious military status didn't seem to enter into the calculations at all. It was good to know that he was on his way back to Utah with a force that looked like a good outfit.

He grimaced a little at the thought, faintly derisive of his own attitude. Getting soft, he thought, just because there was now a chance that a fat-headed War Department might consider his case for ten years and then offer to reinstate him as a second lieutenant!

The thought was not convincing. He did not propose to accept a commission if it were offered. He was not interested. This was simply a matter of giving due respect to a show of military efficiency. Here the army had shaken off its lethargy to do a decent job in a prompt manner. The beef herds were adequate and had been gathered quickly. The expedition was on the march even earlier than he had anticipated. And Marcy had not been superceded by some greenhorn with a year or two of plush-lined seniority.

The alignment of the column told its own story. Two companies of mounted infantry fanned out between the beef herds and the drove of fifteen hundred horses and mules which followed. Squads of mounted riflemen covered the flanks beyond the drovers while two more companies of infantry were spaced along the line of freight wagons which brought up the rear. It was too bad Harney and Van Vliet couldn't be on hand to see how a column should be handled!

He found Marcy at the rear of the column checking with a lieutenant who had taken charge of clearing the camp. "Everything moving in fine style, Captain," he reported.

"We'll try to keep it that way," Marcy said shortly. "There's word of trouble. From Utah."

"You mean the Mormons have attacked?"

Marcy's grin was fleeting. "Stop worrying about her," he laughed. "I didn't put it just the way I meant it. We had a dispatch this morning to the effect that the Mormons know about us and propose to head us off."

"That's to be expected — but how did you get a dispatch through?"

"One of those peculiarities of United States government and geography. Mail service between Salt Lake and California has never been suspended, in spite of the Mormon declaration of war. A message sent to

California in December was relayed to me here. You'd better tell your men."

"No hurry. Let 'em get broken in easily. The Mormons will have a supply problem of their own, so we don't need to worry about an attack until we get reasonably close to Fort Bridger — and that won't be for a couple of months at best."

Marcy nodded. "Handle it your own way. I'd suggest, however, that you pick two or three men and keep them with you most of the time. If you need to send any word back along the column to me use a man who knows as much as possible."

"Good idea. By the time we reach the Arkansas I'll know who to use. Until then it's not likely I'll have anything to tell you."

It turned out to be a good prediction. The column made slow but steady progress, having to suit their pace to the beef herds which could do little more than eight miles a day. There was a little rain but mostly the weather remained fair and the men began to look upon the whole show as a huge picnic. Spencer saw to it that his scouts did not adopt such an attitude. Each day he worked them diligently, shutting off any protests by reminders of what had happened to the main expedition. They were not hard to convince.

At the end of a month they had covered more than a third of the necessary distance. The advance guard had passed Fontaine-qui-bouille Creek and was headed due north with Pike's Peak looming in the northwest. Then a familiar figure appeared ahead and Cal Trent swung his battered cap in salute.

Spencer knew an instant of apprehension but controlled himself to wait for the scout to reach him. Trent was brief, as usual. "Got some dispatches fer Cap Marcy," he greeted. "Ain't lost him, have ye?"

Before Spencer could reply one of his men hailed him and he turned to see a uniformed rider coming up from the rear. "Getting busy around here," he commented. "I thought it was too peaceful to last."

Trent waited in silence until the soldier ranged his horse beside Spencer. "Cap'n Marcy wants ye," the man announced. "Orders are to halt here. Have your men form a picket line."

"Trouble?" Spencer asked, puzzled.

"I reckon not. Express just caught up with us. You'd better git on back right away."

He wheeled his horse and galloped away, leaving Spencer to issue the necessary orders to the three men who were acting as his lieutenants. It happened that two of them were corporals and one was a private, but rank was overlooked in the scout squadron. When the trio spread out to pass the word, Spencer and Trent headed toward the rear. "Mail service is getting mighty active," Spencer commented.

It turned out that Trent had ridden down from Fort Laramie. His dispatches from Marcy had been turned over to a courier at that point and he had been sent back with others. For the most part they contained information about a relief force that was leaving Laramie for Fort Bridger with men and supplies, but there was also a warning about preparations the Mormons were supposed to be making for the interception of Marcy's column. There was no direct word from the camp on Black's Fork.

They found Captain Marcy in close conference with several other officers and a short, squatty plainsman who looked slightly uneasy at his own important status.

"We're ordered to wait here," Marcy announced a bit glumly. "Somebody seems to be worried about us and we're not to move northward until we get reinforcements."

Spencer motioned toward Trent. "Cal just rode in from Laramie with a hint of the same thing. He claims the government is making quite a fuss about getting this mess cleaned up."

"Seems that way," Marcy agreed. "My orders are from General Garland, commanding the Department of New Mexico, but he seems to be passing on the idea from Leavenworth. Major General Smith is to march from the Missouri as quickly as possible. He will take full command with Harney handling one division while Johnston takes the other. Apparently the Mormons are to be taught a real lesson."

Spencer did not voice the thought which had come into his mind. It was good to know that an adequate force was being gathered for the purpose in view, but he could not help thinking about the injustices perpetrated by army red tape. Colonel Johnston had done a remarkable job of salvaging something from the wreckage left by Harney's blundering. He deserved the command of the enlarged expedition but he was to be simply a division commander, on a par with Harney. Perhaps something of the sort would happen to

Captain Marcy. Now that he had done the hard part of the job he would probably find some ranking officer coming along with the reinforcements to rob him of his success.

The expedition spent three weeks along Fontaine-qui-bouille Creek, loafing in pleasant weather while Marcy and Spencer fretted about the waste of time. The supply train from Fort Laramie might have started on time but just as likely it had been delayed. Meanwhile, the army on Black's Fork was waiting for food.

On the twenty-ninth of April a half company of mounted riflemen appeared in camp, bringing orders which made it clear that this was the reinforcement for which three weeks had been wasted. Marcy swore under his breath and ordered an immediate advance. The armchair generals were up to their old tricks.

On the following day the fine spring weather fled before a sudden onslaught of belated winter, the heavy snowfall offering no choice but to halt once more. In two days a good three feet of snow blanketed the entire region and at the height of the storm a part of the mule herd stampeded and ran fifty miles before the howling gale. Infantrymen were quickly added to the line of herders restraining the rest of the stock while Spencer and Trent went out with the scout detachment and a dozen cowboys to recover the mules.

The task required almost a week, but when they returned the ground was getting bare in spots, the spring sun dissipating the intense cold which had accompanied the freak storm.

Marcy had the train ready and as soon as the runaway mules were restored to their proper position the column moved out again. Men were grim again now, the violent blizzard having taken most of the humor out of them. It was as though the elements had contrived this unseasonal storm as a sort of warning. The mountain country ahead was a hard one where plenty of danger still lurked. Men could not content themselves with a bit of brief sunshine. Spring could be treacherous — and so could the mountains.

For several days that reminder was repeated dramatically. In every valley they found the carcasses of antelope that had frozen to death in the snowbanks. Spencer had never heard of such a thing happening before and it brought his worries back. The unlucky animals had counted too heavily on the appearance of spring. Perhaps something of the same nature had happened in the mountains to the north. The partial opening of the trails might even have encouraged Ruth to start the journey east.

Such thoughts haunted him throughout the month of May even though spring was now full upon the land, offering the sort of balmy weather that made it difficult to remember the freezing days. The column forged ahead at an amazing rate. The first of June it hit the banks of Green River some distance south of the Lombard crossing. There had been no sign of Mormon scouts and no further word of the other columns which were known to be converging on Fort Bridger.

Two men from Marcy's old scout company found them the following day and Spencer was able to take a deep breath for the first time in a month. The camp on Black's Fork had wintered well, as had the stock camp to the south. The army was making final preparations for the march on Utah, waiting only for the supply train which was known to be approaching the upper crossing of the Green. The Mormons had withdrawn their militia and were not making any known preparations for resistance to the enlarged force that was soon to be thrown against them.

One of the scouts even knew about Ruth Corliss and reported that she was quite well. Marcy seemed to read Spencer's mind, for he grinned sympathetically and said, "You'd better go on ahead, Dan. We'll not need you from this point on. Give her my best."

Spencer did not need any urging.

CHAPTER NINETEEN

The encampment on Black's Fork — camp Scott, they were calling it now — was a scene of confusion when Spencer rode in late the following day. Most of the troop units had already moved out, but most of the wagons were still in their rectangles, awaiting the horses and mules being brought in to move them. He could see that repairs had been made and that axles had been greased, but otherwise the camp had an air of indolence. He had expected the bustle and excitement to be found where an army is preparing to launch an offensive. Instead he found teamsters sleeping in the sun, a couple of supply sergeants browbeating a reluctant work detail — and four troopers hiding behind a pile of freight to play cards.

He stopped to ask directions of one of the sergeants and learned that the Fifth was now at Bridger preparing to march into Echo Canyon. The troops would move on Utah within the next day or two, the wagons when and if stock arrived to pull them. The sergeant made it all sound pretty dreary.

"Any sign that the Mormons will resist?" Spencer asked, puzzled at the general tone of the camp.

"Why the hell should they?" the sergeant snapped. Then he went back to cursing the reluctant soldiers.

Spencer elected not to become involved in any more of this conversation. At the moment he was not very much concerned about why the camp was glum and slipshod. Nor was he particularly interested in the ill-humors of supply sergeants. Finding Ruth Corliss was his only immediate concern and he didn't intend to let the happy prospect be dimmed by anything else.

He found Gabe Peace at the new camp of the Fifth. The sergeant took him to headquarters at once. There was time only for a few questions from Peace about the Taos expedition and then he was shaking hands with Major Pierce and a lieutenant whose name he did not remember. This time he had to tell his story in great detail, prompt questions jogging him whenever he skipped through any part of it. They were pleased to know that Marcy was coming through, but they seemed much more interested in the story of Donnel and Garcia. That seemed odd, Spencer thought. Officers planning an invasion ought to be more interested in their supplies.

Suddenly he broke it off with a short laugh. "Let the rest of it keep. Where's Ruth?"

Pierce looked surprised. "I thought Gabe had told you. She left for Kansas three days ago."

"Here we go again!" Spencer growled. "I've spent half of my life chasing around trying to catch up with folks." Then he laughed. "Maybe if I sit right down here and sulk she'll come back again."

The two officers exchanged glances and then looked at Sergeant Peace to see if he could explain this crazy talk. The sergeant shook his head and Spencer chuckled. "So I sound loco. Let me tell you how I finally caught up with Garcia. I skipped that part before."

When he had completed the yarn Pierce shook his head. "You make yourself sound almost as futile as we feel. Have you heard the latest on our orders?"

"I haven't heard anything. A man with half an eye could see that nobody's very enthusiastic around this camp, but I didn't know why."

"I can tell you. The government has let us down again. About a week ago a commissioner passed through here on the way to Utah. He carried a proclamation from President Buchanan which offers full pardon to all of the Mormons providing they offer no further resistance. We haven't heard any official reply yet but we know that all of their militia has been withdrawn and one of our scouts came to tell us that he'd talked with your friend McGee out there in the hills. According to McGee they have already received their orders to go home and stay there."

"What's wrong with that?" Spencer asked. "This army started out to occupy Utah peacefully. At least that was the way they told it. Now you're in position to do the very thing you started out to do."

"Don't talk like a fool! How much authority will Federal officials ever have in Salt Lake when the Mormons are laughing up their sleeves, remembering how their plow-jockeys made fools of this army? They'll feel that we are in Utah simply because they allowed us to be. Our men are going to resent it and they'll hunt for excuses to get back at the people who forced them to spend such a miserable winter. I'd rather fight it out now and have a clear-cut peace."

Spencer nodded. "I can see your point. What makes me wonder is the way this whole thing got tangled up. The President must have been issuing his peace proclamation at the same time that he was sending men and supplies for a full-scale invasion. Was he playing it safe or was he just confused?"

"I think that one is obvious enough. The whole government is confused. They don't know what to do about Kansas and they never did have a sensible idea about Utah. Anyone who was with us last summer knows that. At least three officers of this regiment are planning to resign their commissions this summer rather than to serve under such a government."

Spencer tried to change the subject but Major Pierce was not to be halted. Clearly he was blowing off steam that had been pent up for some time. "I'm a New Englander," he went on, "and we like the idea of a good solid government in Washington. We don't think this country can get along without it. Buchanan is playing right into the hands of men who want to split it. He's destroying its prestige to the point where men with pride think of their state citizenship in preference to claiming any part of the bungling mess in Washington. If the southerners should force a showdown over this Kansas issue, we'd see a lot of good officers pulling out to stay with their states. The army would split wide open."

"I can understand that," Spencer agreed. "I've been thinking about Colonel Johnston in that respect."

"*General* Johnston now," Pierce corrected, "but you're right. He's a Kentuckian and he has every reason in the world to be disgusted with the administration. I could guess what he would do if we came to a crisis." He broke off suddenly and asked, "What about you? Are you planning to take that commission if it's offered to you?"

"No. I'm like you. I don't want to see this country break up — but I don't have any desire to go back into a service that is controlled by a lot of crazy men in Washington. Now forget politics and tell me about Ruth. Who is she traveling with and how did it happen that she left?"

"Sorry. I let myself get out of hand. Miss Corliss is riding with Captain Hawes and his wife. Last week the captain was ordered back to Kansas for some sort of special duty. He had to do some fast figuring but he managed to get a wagon and six reasonably fit mules. His travel orders naturally did not include his wife because she wasn't officially supposed to be with him. That made it awkward but we worked out a plan. Miss Corliss, as registered owner of wagons that had been destroyed by Mormons, put in a claim for a wagon to replace one of hers. We put a bit of pressure on our friend Captain Burns, who has been trying to get himself back in the good graces of the command, and he signed a paper which let her have a wagon and a team. When we learned of the Mormon pardon nobody cared very much about equipment anyway."

Spencer grinned. "The army takes care of its own," he said.

"But sometimes in some remarkably perverse ways," Pierce added. "Now let's see if we can't get you outfitted a little better for the next stage of your chase. If you don't mind my being frank, you are much too dirty and bewhiskered to set out on the trail of a lady who left such romantic messages behind her."

"What messages?"

"Never mind. You'll be catching her within a few days. Let her deliver them in person. It'll be a lot more fun."

The few days Pierce referred to proved to be almost two weeks. Leaving Fort Bridger the next morning with a clean face and well-scrubbed buckskins, Spencer was just in time to meet Captain Marcy and a pair of scouts riding ahead of the train from Taos. The meeting delayed him for nearly three hours while they exchanged information and said their farewells. Then a wet snow overtook him at the crossing of the Green and he had to lose a full day when the trails became too slippery for progress.

Only one day later he encountered Colonel Hoffman's supply train coming west from Laramie and again there was a long delay. Hoffman wanted information about the peace offer to Utah and the possible threat of Mormon raiders. Only at the end of the talk did he realize Spencer's identity. Then he did some talking on his own account. Apparently the story of the Taos expedition had become well known already, growing in the retelling until it had been shaped to resemble a real romance. Disgraced officer with a grudge against the army had remembered his duty and saved Marcy's detachment from death in the mountains — just in time to clear his name and be a hero. It was all pretty sickening and Spencer got himself away just as soon as he possibly could.

It made him wonder, however, as he sent his horse east along Pacific Creek. Just what had his motives actually been in following Marcy's men? Had he simply been concerned about a man who had come to be a good friend? Had he acted merely to thwart Curt Donnel? Had it been a sympathetic feeling for soldiers who had volunteered for what was considered an impossible task? It was vaguely disturbing that he was not able to answer any of those queries.

Finally he forced the whole thing from his mind and concentrated on thoughts of the girl who was somewhere along the trail ahead of him. It was much more pleasant to remember her pert features and blonde hair than it was to grouse about the idiotic antics of an army commanded by blundering politicos.

He found the wagon halted at the Big Sandy crossing, waiting for the swollen stream to subside a little after the melting of the last wet snow. Ruth saw him coming and ran down the trail to meet him.

Suddenly he swung from his horse and stood stock-still while the girl covered the last few feet between them. The act was just odd enough for her to hesitate as he was about to put his arms around her.

"Is something wrong?" she asked quietly, some of the happiness going out of her eyes.

He pulled her to him and held her tight. "Not a thing," he assured her. "That was just my new strategy. Nowadays I wait."

She looked up in perplexity but he silenced her question with a kiss. "I'll tell you all about it pretty soon. We'll have from here to Kansas to do our talking."

"Just talking?" she murmured, keeping her eyes down.

"Silent Spencer, they used to call me," he chuckled. "I can keep my mouth shut when there are better things to do."

She kissed him again and swung around to take his arm as they headed toward the waiting couple at the wagon. "Come along now," she said gaily. "I want you to meet Captain and Mrs. Hawes."

"I hope he's not a quartermaster officer," he said in a low voice. "I don't seem to get along with 'em very well."

Her laugh bubbled up then. "Didn't Captain Marcy or Major Pierce tell you? I practically asked the major to make it clear."

He remembered the grin Pierce had worn when refusing to pass on Ruth's message. "Nobody told me anything," he grumbled.

She was introducing him then. "Folks, I want you to meet Dan Spencer. Dan, this is Mrs. Hawes, a very fine lady, and this is her husband, Captain Hawes, recently regimental chaplain of the Tenth Infantry."

The words which wanted to come to Spencer's tongue would not have been proper greetings to use in addressing a chaplain and his wife. Mostly they concerned the perverse nature of an adjutant named Pierce. Fortunately he was able to restrain them. He did not say a word until the first greetings were over. Then he reached out to pull the girl back into the crook of his arm. "Padre," he said quietly. "Have you got your Book handy?"

Captain Hawes showed his surprise. "So soon?" he asked.

"It's already late," Spencer told him solemnly. "Almost a year ago a fellow named Callahan practically had us married. It's time we made an honest man of him."

"Nothing for us, you understand," Ruth said, her tone a careful imitation of Spencer's. "Just for the sake of Callahan's reputation."

Mrs. Hawes proved to be a woman of understanding. "Don't gape, Henry," she said. "Get the Book."